In Harm's Way

ISBN: 978-1-0693045-6-8

Created with Atticus

For D.

Chapter One

H e wasn't going to get away this time. When Detective Luce Allen returned to work on a Friday afternoon, she didn't expect her case to break wide open. She was grateful it did, the buzzing activity around her a welcome distraction.

Joe Danes had been on their radar for some time, suspected of posing as a teenager online and luring underage girls into the house he had inherited from his mother.

Getting to her feet, Luce gripped the edge of her desk, the pain stealing her breath for a second. That might actually be her fault, as she hadn't taken the time to rest as recommended by her doctor. She had to be here, at least, to be sure everything went according to plan.

It didn't matter that she wasn't going to be there for the arrest. Her colleagues were more than capable, and within the next few hours, Danes would no longer present a danger to young girls. Luce had few illusions about the larger impact. There would be others in his place.

All she wanted for the day was to bring Ashley Thompson home, take that win she hoped was coming on the heels of months-long work. She'd worry about the rest another day.

She sat back down and opened the top drawer, searching for a bottle of pills she knew was there.

"Allen, are you coming?"

So much for trying to stay under the radar. She cast a glance from Detective Ritter to Lieutenant Chomsky who was standing in the doorway of her office, following the exchange.

Luce made the decision in a split second. Danes was a sleaze, possibly a sex offender. He was also oblivious to the consequences coming his way. This should be over soon, and she could still make it an early night. Come in tomorrow morning, take Sunday. A couple of days, the doctor had said. She would be following orders, sort of.

"Okay, sure."

Ritter gave her a strange look. Luce couldn't blame him. They weren't close, and of course he wasn't privy to her internal reasoning.

"Ritter, Allen, we're still on track?" Chomsky might be calmer and more soft-spoken than any boss Luce had ever had, but she was also a no-nonsense kind of person.

"We're good," Luce said as she slipped the Kevlar on. "Let's go get him."

With everything they had learned about Danes, they had no indication that he was armed. He wasn't the type to rig his front door, or anything of the kind. It would be all right.

She had wanted distraction. She got her wish.

Luce took her own car rather than catch a ride with Ritter. She didn't think he was expecting anything else. They had prepared for this day, all the information in place. Neither of them was much into filling the time with small talk.

She spent the twenty-minute drive going over the next steps in her head, relieved that she would be a part of this bust after all. It would be a win. It had to be.

She parked on the other side of the street from the two-story house to where they'd followed the signal of Ashley's phone.

In addition, they had recovered private conversations between Ashely and *shyguy15* and found out they had made plans to meet eleven days ago, the day Ashley vanished. Initially, Luce had used the pseudonym *cait2309*, succeeding into baiting Danes, but with the evidence they had against him, they no longer needed her to pretend.

Luce joined Ritter who was standing to the side of the gate, conferring with one of the uniformed officers.

"Want to do the honors?" he asked.

She straightened her shoulders and walked up to the front door. *Shyguy15* was about to learn that *cait2309* was in fact a thirty-four-year-old woman, and she wasn't playing.

She reached out and rang the doorbell, a melodic sound echoing in the entryway. Silence followed.

If he tried to flee, he would run straight into the officers waiting for him at the back entrance. There was nowhere to go for Joe Danes. She rang the bell again, then pounded on the door.

A whole lot of nothing.

"We're going in," she decided. "What? We have the arrest warrant. Ashley's phone is in this house. What are we waiting for?"

"Allen. Take a breath. Give me one second."

She waited, on pins and needles, frustrated with him, and herself, as he made the call. It took all her self-restraint not to start pacing. Luce had to admit he was right. Danes couldn't go anywhere. They had to execute the steps in the right order—anything else would be a disservice to Ashley, and the other girls.

Ritter ended the call and checked something else on his phone before he said, "Got the green light. Either way, Danes will be in for a surprise."

They both stepped back while the entrance was breached.

Luce had a sinking feeling in the pit of her stomach. She hoped it was merely a reflection of her overall state of mind, or even the fact that she'd been willing to rush procedure to save a young girl.

She knew herself better than that, and her instincts rarely betrayed her. The first floor had a kitchen, a living area, and a half bath. There were dishes in the sink that had remnants of food stuck to them. Eggs.

"Detective? There's no one upstairs," one of the officers told her.

Luce nodded, her attention drawn to a door underneath the stairs leading to the upper floor, almost camouflaged by the paint. She reached out and opened it, revealing a narrow staircase.

"Christ," she heard Ritter say, the single word chilling her. The possibilities had multiplied in a heartbeat, and none of them were good. Keeping her hand on her weapon, she inched down the sparsely lit stairs that ended in a space barely big enough for one person to stand, and another door. It wasn't locked. Obviously, Danes didn't care if they, or anyone, found it. She drew a sharp breath and turned the knob.

It looked like Danes had been waiting for them after all: The only splash of color in the dingy, dark bedroom was a red backpack. To no one's surprise, Ashley's cell phone was inside.

❦

It wasn't nothing, she had to remind herself of that. Evidence put Ashley into that house, and it was likely that DNA recovered from Danes's place would help them advance other cases.

Still, as she sat over what little they had on paper at this moment, nauseated from too much coffee, Luce couldn't help feeling defeated.

No body. No worst-case scenario. It didn't look good though.

"You've done everything you could for today. Why don't you go home?"

She looked up at the lieutenant who had stopped at Luce's desk on her way out. Chomsky had a point. Everyone she was waiting on had probably left already. Danes's photo had gone out to the press. The rest...If they were lucky, they'd have some results tomorrow, probably not in the early morning.

"You know, I think I'll do that. I'll see you tomorrow."

Chomsky lingered for a few seconds before she said, "Bright and early. Good night, Allen."

Luce had multiple reasons not to walk out with her. The few minutes it would take to get to the parking garage might require small talk. This wasn't a good time. She waited a few more minutes, gathered her coat and keys and left as well.

Chapter Two

S ometime a few months ago, Luce had decided it would be a good idea to update parts of the house she had owned for three years. She had no particular reason other than perhaps watching too many reno shows during her off time, and so she made a budget, assessed what she'd be able to do herself and what she'd need help with.

Her enthusiasm had been wavering lately, and it was at an all-time low when she returned home only to find a note from her neighbor. *I waited, but no one showed up today.*

Luce let out a curse, and then another. Somewhere, somebody had to be laughing at her plans so hard they had to be near apoplectic. The Universe? Inside the house, she walked through the parts still deep in renovations, where she had imagined a beautiful wide-open space, kitchen, dining, living area. All she could see were open walls, dust, and plastic tarps, and not a whole lot of progress.

Kind of like the case—or the rest of her life. She walked back to the more civilized part that housed her bedroom and main bath. Those were on the list as well. Luce leaned her forehead against the wall. At least she had the foresight not to do everything at once, but the gratitude for that fact carried her only so far.

She wanted a hot bath, but she couldn't do that either, not yet. A shower would have to suffice, and after that...perhaps food. Her stomach hadn't settled yet. She might just go to bed and meet her colleagues and boss bright and early the next day.

Halfway through the next steps, Luce changed her mind, deciding to swallow her pride. It was better than spending a sleepless night wondering where Ashley might be, or if she was still alive.

Her hair was still damp when she called the number, something, Luce admitted, she should have done yesterday—or the day before. Would it have made any difference?

"Luce, hi. Are you okay?"

"Yes, I'm fine," she hurried to say. "I was wondering if you could use some company." That was an odd way to word it, but she was confident that Kendra would understand. Somehow, she always did.

"Are you reading my mind? More importantly, have you eaten yet? Scratch that, I'm pretty sure you haven't. I have pasta on the stove and tiramisu in the fridge. How does that sound?"

"Like heaven," Luce said, embarrassed at the swell of emotion. She hadn't cried once this week, and she wasn't planning on doing it now. She was doing fine.

"Good. I'll see you in twenty?"

"Maybe less." On the other end of the line, Kendra laughed softly. Her voice sounded more sober when she said, "I'm glad you called. This week has been wild."

"No kidding."

As she drove over to Kendra's, Luce went over a few rehearsed lines in case her friend wanted to talk but abandoned them before she arrived. Kendra was the most intuitive, least judgmental person Luce had ever met. If she offered pasta and dessert, that was all that was on the table for this Friday night, unless Luce decided otherwise.

She was tired. A meal and perhaps a bed in a place that wasn't a construction site would do wonders for her state of mind.

Kendra greeted her at the door, pulling her into a brief and bearable hug.

"Hey. Come on in."

"Thanks for having me."

"Of course."

Luce had to smile at the set-up. Even a spontaneous late-night dinner came with a nicely set table in the dining room. Kendra had a bottle of red wine on the table.

"One sip doesn't harm, though I know you—"

"No, thank you." The scents from the kitchen had woken her appetite, though Luce rarely drank. "It's been a long day," she added. "One of those that make me wish I liked it more."

Kendra's gaze lingered, concerned. She poured a glass of water for both of them.

"I thought you were going to take a couple of days?"

"I'm fine. I'll tell you more if you give me some of that pasta."

"Coming right up."

Giving Luce the last opportunity to stall, Kendra went over to the kitchen counter to fill their plates. Yes, she could have taken a couple of days. Such was the privilege that came with her paycheck, and its benefits. Luce had no rational explanation other than her unfinished project—projects—paining her. Being a restless person by nature.

She couldn't know that there would be any development in Danes's case.

Kendra returned with their plates, and they started eating.

"I'm sorry," Kendra said. "I was going to call you, but I worked late every night, and, well, I thought you might be resting. I should have known better."

"I got your text."

"So...How are you?"

Luce shrugged. "I told you. Okay. I haven't been doing any heavy lifting. No surprises, no complications. I'm more pissed that the asshole who locked a fifteen-year-old in his basement got away. With her."

Kendra winced, but her tone was calm. "You'll find her."

Yes. Eventually. So much damage would already be done. Luce knew that she didn't have to spell it out for Kendra.

"We will. It would have been better if it had happened tonight."

"Yeah." Her pensive tone suggested to Luce she was thinking about her own work that, too, was often time-sensitive when it came to avoiding trauma. Worse trauma. Men like Danes always stood in the way. "One way or another, you deserve a time-out."

"Says the woman who's home late every night."

"You may have a point. It's easier to give advice than to take it. And speaking of which, you know if you have any questions..."

"Thank you, but the doctor told me everything." Truth be told, she had drifted occasionally, but she'd caught the most important parts. "Don't worry. I'm taking care of myself. I'm not ashamed or anything. No regrets. I just got bored at home."

Kendra searched her gaze, obviously satisfied with what she saw. "Okay. Tell me about your renovation, then."

Luce shook her head. "If I didn't know you better, I'd think you're trying to make me cry."

"That bad?"

"I'm not sure. Perhaps I should have spent that time trying to get somebody on the phone rather than work...Didn't you promise me tiramisu?"

"I did, and I always keep my promises." Kendra got up, gently touching her shoulder. "I'll make us some coffee."

Luce had known Kendra only a little over a year, but already she had made a big difference in her life. She'd never had a friend like her, someone she could talk to if she needed to, and be silent with. Passionate conversations about politics and long-term solutions, and movie nights with ice cream. It was everything she had ever hoped for in a friendship, and tonight, it was the only thing that kept her on track.

Once upon a time, she might have thought that there could be more, but what they had was something so rare she couldn't afford to lose it. She simply didn't want to go back to a time before Kendra in her life.

That was why she always told her the truth. Tonight was no exception. She could handle this unexpected detour. She didn't regret her choice to have an abortion.

Luce was determined to do her job. At some point in the future, those renovations would be done as well. She had a sleepless night after all, but it was much better in Kendra's king size bed than it would have been in her own house where memories and questions still took up considerable room.

Dr. Bradley had mentioned something about sexual activity too, but he didn't need to worry. Luce had no intention of engaging in said activities, with anyone, for some time to come.

Before she slipped into a light sleep, she wondered when this comfortable arrangement would come to an end...probably when Kendra started dating again. The relief she felt knowing that Kendra had been too busy to even think about, made her feel guilty. But she appreciated the warm soft sheets, and the company, even though there was enough space for them not to touch at any time of the night.

⬥

By the time she had taken another shower and dressed, Kendra had already set the table in the kitchen. Luce cast a glance at her watch. She hadn't received any message from the department, so she assumed she'd have time for breakfast. It would be a shame to let those eggs, bacon, and fluffy buttery croissants go to waste.

She pushed the image of eggs sticking to a plate in another house from her mind. No news meant good news. She had to believe that.

"Why aren't you married?" she asked after taking a first sip of the perfectly brewed coffee.

"Oh, I don't know," Kendra answered, her tone wistful. "The woman of my dreams hasn't asked me yet."

What did that mean? How much had she missed being so focused on her own issues?

"Are you seeing someone? Why didn't you tell me?"

Any future overnight stays would likely be in Kendra's guest room. She should be happy for her, right? Anything else would be petty.

"No, I'm not dating anyone," Kendra clarified, and Luce suppressed a relieved sigh. "Everyone I work with is married, and you know I barely leave the place. Going out with patients would be frowned upon, so no, there's nobody."

"I'd like to discuss your questionable sense of humor some more, but I'm afraid I don't have that much time."

Kendra took another sip of her coffee. "And I'd like to chastise you for going to work, but that might be hypocritical, so I won't. But no heavy lifting yet, you hear me?"

"What do you think I do over there?" Luce asked, amused despite herself. "I'll spend most of my time with paperwork and waiting on more paperwork." Come to think of it, there was nothing humorous about the situation. "I swear I'll take it easy, but with the way this case is going, I doubt there's an opportunity for anything else."

"If you want, I could come over on Sunday, take a look at the construction site."

"You know anything about construction?"

"I might have more hidden talents you don't know about..."

It might sound like flirting. Luce was aware that Kendra's intention was more likely to check on her, but either way, she'd take it.

Chapter Three

Luce got a call from Ritter before she could make it to the station.

"Ashley?" she asked, her breath catching in her throat. Luce was unsure of her capability to handle any more bad news. She needed things to head in the right direction from now on.

"No," he said. "Husband reported his wife missing. Wendy Tillis, twenty-nine, went to a doctor's appointment yesterday, never returned. None of their friends or family have heard anything. I'm on my way. Meet me there?"

"Okay. I'll see you soon."

The address he texted her was about ten minutes away from her location, an area with many older apartment buildings. Half of them had been recently converted into condos, the fate of the rest still unclear.

At least they weren't dealing with the worst-case scenario. Yet.

Ritter was waiting for her outside the building that housed the Tillises' apartment. She noted that the lobby and hallway looked clean, if dated. The elevator worked, but made a funny, worry-inducing noise at the end.

Luce was used to Ritter not talking more than the necessary. When they got off on the sixth floor, he said, "Stairs on the way down."

She had no objection.

"Thank you so much for coming," Steve Tillis greeted them at the door. "I didn't know what else to do...no one has seen Wendy or heard from her."

"We're going to figure this out," Ritter assured him as they followed the distraught man into the apartment and a modestly furnished but cozy living room. "You said your wife went to a doctor's appointment? Where?"

Luce caught a glance of the box resting against the wall, the realization of what it contained coming with an onslaught of mixed emotions. This was urgent. Ashley's case, they all were.

Wendy and her husband had purchased a crib.

"At the Women's Health Center. She was there for a check-up," Steve Tillis said. "I called them, and they told me she saw the doctor. She left...and that's the last time anyone saw her. You must find her!"

Luce exchanged a look with Ritter, wondering what he was thinking. She, too, could think of various scenarios.

"Are you aware of any news she might have gotten during that appointment?" Difficult news, something that might have made her want to hide from her husband?

"No. I usually go with her, and I'm her emergency contact. They would have called me if they thought...everything was fine!" His eyes were welling up.

Luce was human enough to be touched by his obvious devastation. She was cynical enough to be aware he could be faking. It wouldn't be the first time she was confronted with a scenario like that.

"We'll have to talk to her doctor," she said. "Could you give us their name?"

"It's Dr. Martin," Tillis answered, and Luce breathed a sigh of relief. Not Kendra. Not Dr. Bradley she had seen last Thursday. Any of those possibilities would have caused unnecessary complications going forward.

"Okay. And you said you usually join her? Why not this time?"

"I wish I had." His voice broke. "I can't believe this is happening! We were so happy about this baby. I wanted to go with her because of those protesters, but I had to work an extra shift."

The returning group with a varying number of people, brandishing signs and slurs in front of the clinic was a constant subject of conversation between Luce and Kendra. Employees often received threats, some more serious than others.

She had first met Kendra while investigating a credible bomb threat at the clinic, one they could never tie to the people out front.

One of them might have spoken to Wendy Tillis, threatened her or worse—or they presented a convenient scapegoat for Mr. Tillis. Just because the memory of getting yelled at only a few days ago made her blood pressure rise, it didn't mean she wasn't looking at all the angles.

"I'm sure your employer can confirm that?" Ritter asked.

"Yes, of course." Tillis made a dismissive gesture. "I know you have to ask that, but a dozen people saw me there, and there are cameras."

"We'll get the information about your wife out there," Luce promised. "Let's go over the timeline again. When did you realize she was missing?"

"I called her from work to let her know I couldn't make it." He held out his phone. "I left her a message. When I left work this morning, I realized she never called me back. She wasn't home either, so I checked with the clinic, and they said she'd been there yesterday afternoon. I started calling around, but no one had seen her."

Luce took notes as he spoke.

"I'd like you to come to the station with us. We can record your statement, and we'll let you know as soon as we learn anything."

"Of course. Thank you, Detective." He wiped a hand over his face. "There's a logical explanation, right? Maybe she just got a little overwhelmed, needs a time-out."

"Has that ever happened before?" Luce asked, a sense of alarm gripping her. "Her, leaving without telling anyone where she was going?"

"No. Never. I don't know why I said that. We both really wanted that baby, but it's been tough. Financially. And I know she was nervous about seeing the doctor, because of those people always yelling at her. They don't even listen. Wendy would never have an abortion. She could never do anything like that."

It was the absolute worst timing for the cramping to return. Luce noticed that she'd been doing much better after spending some time with Kendra, not a surprise. In any case, she'd had worse.

Financial difficulties. A small discrepancy. She had to focus. Interesting though not surprising that Mr. Tillis seemed to agree with the protesters on the matter. They might have to come back to that.

"We should go," she said. "The sooner we can get moving, the better."

⁘

Before they went to Chomsky's office to update her on the progress, Ritter took her aside.

"Are you okay?" he asked. "You looked a little pale in there for a moment."

"I'm good." Luce cast a glance at her phone. "I was hoping we'd have news on Ashley by lunch," she said with a sigh. "Let's go do this."

Lieutenant Chomsky listened as they related their conversation with Steve Tillis.

"He mentioned financial troubles," Ritter said. "We can't rule him out yet. He's nervous. We have yet to confirm the alibi."

"I want to set up interviews with the clinic's staff and some of the protesters. They must have seen her, maybe even spoken to her, and that could give us an insight into her state of mind."

"You do that," Lieutenant Chomsky addressed her. "And be careful. Don't react to any provocation."

"Understood," Luce said tersely.

Only yesterday, she thought she could manage to sneak out early in the afternoon. She saw now that she wouldn't be able to get away without giving Chomsky a good reason, something she wanted to avoid.

While Luce had the privilege of being able to stay home, many others didn't. Besides, lives depended on the progress they might make today.

She didn't have to worry. If they ran into Dr. Bradley, he'd have to observe doctor-patient confidentiality, and Kendra wouldn't betray her trust either. Luce would have preferred not to go back so soon, but it had to be done. End of story.

They recorded Tillis's statement first. He didn't waver from the details he had given them before.

After sneaking away for a quick bathroom break and some ibuprofen, Luce felt ready to tackle the next steps, physically, anyway. They took Ritter's car this time.

Since it was the weekend, most people had more time on their hands, including the people harassing women at the clinic. Expectation caused her stomach to clench as they neared the building.

She wasn't afraid or feeling like she owed anyone an explanation. Luce knew she didn't. Knowing what they would run into made her angry, even more than it had those few times she had gone to see Kendra and other witnesses during the other investigation. Even more so these days, regardless of her own experience. She couldn't let them get to her. Luce was aware of that even without Chomsky's warning.

"We show Mrs. Tillis's picture around first?" Ritter suggested.

"Yes. Sure." She had thought they might split up, but it made sense to have another pair of eyes, a witness if necessary.

He parked in the lot, and they walked towards the entrance, making their way through the small crowd. As usual, the attention turned to every newcomer. The lines were the same, predictable, patronizing and disdainful.

Why don't you want to choose life? We can help you. Don't do it. Don't be a murderer. Repent.

Clenching her teeth, Luce wondered how Wendy Tillis must have felt coming here on her own, to get a check-up for a wanted pregnancy.

"I'm Detective Allen, this is Detective Ritter," she said, raising her voice above the chants and shouts, with moderate success. "We have a few questions. Folks. Please. Listen for a moment?" Luce held up the picture that Steve had provided them with, and to her surprise and relief, the two dozen or so people started to quiet down and turn to her. She saw that a couple of them were armed. That was nothing new either. "Thank you. This is Wendy Tillis. She went missing after leaving the clinic yesterday afternoon."

"Perhaps she couldn't live with herself," a woman in her late thirties or early forties, with an elementary school age girl next to her, said.

"Have you seen her? Wendy came for a check-up. It is important that we find her."

Some stepped closer, studying the picture in earnest.

"I hope you're really interested in finding her." The man was in his twenties, carrying a sign.

"What does that mean?" *Don't snap*. Keeping her expression neutral was almost painful.

"You know. For all we know someone's looking for a way to turn this around on us. It wouldn't be the first time we got blamed for someone else's shit."

"The woman is pregnant and missing. If you have any information, I hope it's in line with *your* interests to help us find her. We'd be grateful."

He stared at her, and for a few uncomfortable seconds, Luce wondered if he recognized her. She had made her way straight to the entrance, kept walking no matter how angry those shouts made her. They knew nothing about her, or Wendy Tillis.

"I might have seen her. A check-up, you said? I think I saw her coming out. We tried to talk to her, but she was kind of hysterical."

Before or after you "talked" to her?

"We?"

"A few of us regulars." He pointed to the woman with the child who stood with two men. One of them was the one she'd seen carrying. The other stood out since he was wearing a suit. He looked familiar though Luce couldn't place him.

"I'd like to take your name and contact details in case we need to reach out to you, or anyone else."

"What? No way. I don't know what happened to her!"

"You can help us." Luce forced herself to soften her tone even though the urge to shake him was strong. "Every little detail can be important. What if something happens to her baby? You don't want to be responsible for that, do you?" He wanted to make strangers feel guilty, two could play that game. The difference was the strangers that sought medical help were none of his business, but finding Wendy was Luce's. She didn't mind playing any card she had, especially with Ashley's case still weighing on her.

Chapter Four

They had almost finished talking to Dr. Martin when Kendra passed them by in the hallway, doing a double-take.

"Detective Allen. You're still...working."

Luce gave her a shrug and an apologetic smile.

"My colleague, Detective Ritter. Dr. Jones. We came here once because of a bomb threat." She didn't know why she felt the need to explain this to Ritter who had never asked her a personal question. Her judgment might be a bit off. She hoped that didn't mean she had misread the signs with Tillis. He seemed genuinely afraid for his wife.

It might all be for show, but for all they knew he was about to build a crib. Those men outside the security doors and scanners were carrying guns to intimidate strangers.

"Nice to meet you, Detective. You're here about a patient?"

"Mr. Tillis reported his wife missing," Dr. Martin answered for Luce. "I'm afraid I couldn't help the detectives much. They already knew what I told her husband."

Kendra's eyes narrowed as she, no doubt, made the connection.

"I know you have to come here, but do you have a suspect already?"

That was...blunt.

"I'm sorry, but we can't talk about an ongoing investigation. We are trying to trace Mrs. Tillis's steps from here."

"That makes sense. I hope you find her soon." She hesitated. "Detective Allen, do you have a moment?"

"Of course." Curious about what Kendra might have to tell her, Luce followed her a few steps away from the men. "According to Dr. Martin, Mrs. Tillis saw only him. Did she tell you anything—?"

"Luce."

"If she walked away to be by herself for a bit, that would be the best-case scenario. I'm still waiting on the lab results from Danes' house—"

"Luce, hold on a second."

Something in Kendra's tone made her stop. Anticipating reproach, she held up her hands. "I know. I couldn't anticipate this, but I'll take it easy tonight. I'm okay, I promise. We'll talk tomorrow?"

"Yes, we will. I might have some leftover tiramisu to bring...but only if you take tomorrow off. Seriously. Friend's orders, but I know Dr. Bradley would agree."

"I swear. There's very little I wouldn't do for more of that tiramisu."

"It's a good thing I know the way to your heart."

Did that woman ever.

They shared a smile, understanding that any promises were somewhat conditional on a lack of emergencies and other unexpected incidents. Save for those, Luce could probably stick to hers.

Kendra's words, however, carried more meaning than she was able to admit—especially this week. She needed a friend more than anything.

"He's laughing at us." Luce closed the file with a resounding noise. Across from her, Ritter didn't disagree though he cast a glance at the clock on the wall. They had come back to the station, but unlike Luce, he seemed to have somewhere to be. She ignored the clear hint.

"So, we can put Ashley at Danes's house, that's not exactly big news. How did he know we were coming? How did he get away without anyone noticing?"

"Neighbors keep to themselves," Ritter suggested. "There's none that close anyway. He's not driving his car. He must have been planning his exit for a while."

"Nothing from the lab yet?"

"It's the weekend," he reminded her. "To be honest, I don't expect much before mid-week."

That seemed like an eternity away. A lot could happen until then.

"Okay, Wendy Tillis," she redirected the conversation. "Everything the husband said checks out so far. He was at work. He accompanied Wendy to her previous appointments. I want to talk to the folks outside the clinic some more."

"What good will that do other than they'll claim you harassed them? We'll check out the security cameras. Tillis will be on the evening news. Somebody will have seen her."

Luce didn't share what was on her mind, that he was likely right. Whatever happened to Wendy Tillis, she didn't deserve any of it. That didn't change the fact that more people were likely to pay attention because the missing woman was attractive, young and white.

She hoped it wouldn't be too late for either her or Ashley. Days like this she dreamed of quitting the job and flipping houses instead. She had a good eye for design, one of the contractors had told her. Now she couldn't reach them on the phone. The cases were piling up on her desk.

She couldn't seem to win.

"We have to keep an eye on them," she said anyway. "Gut feeling."

"I'm not ruling them out, but I think the D.A. will ask for a bit more than a hunch," Ritter returned dryly. "Let's call it a day. They'll let us know if anything happens."

As much as she hated to accept the inevitable, not wanting to face Kendra's wrath was the bigger motivation. That, and the promised leftover dessert. Speaking of which, she could buy Kendra's favorite coffee for tomorrow, and tonight's dinner, on her way home.

❦

Taking it easy. She was, sitting at her kitchen table in PJs and a robe, a new pot of coffee brewing while she finished the old one. Pizza for dinner—someday soon, Luce would get back to a healthier lifestyle, but she had other priorities at the moment. Ashley. Wendy. Around their names, she had written down the various theories. In Ashley's case, the suspect and his motive where clear.

As for Wendy's, Luce knew that Ritter and Chomsky were leaning a different way, and perhaps there had been some sort of conflict between husband and wife. About finances. About the pregnancy even. When he mentioned the possibility of Wendy simply taking time for herself, and then claimed it had never happened before—was it intentional? To create the idea Wendy might be dealing with mental issues?

Luce wasn't yet ready to doubt his story, but she had to admit they couldn't completely rule him out. Statistics spoke a clear language.

In her mind, she wandered back to the short interactions with the protesters. They had sort of come around when they realized the missing woman had no intention of having an abortion, but they didn't know that when they first saw Wendy Tillis, or, apparently, even after she had left the clinic.

Luce got up to pour the cold coffee into the sink and get herself a fresh cup. She stared at the paper, recalling the short walk from the parking lot to the front door, the atmosphere brimming with hostility and the threat of violence.

A group of them had been showing up at the clinic for as long as she could remember. The current constellation felt emboldened by the Supreme Court's decision, hoping that a federal ban was in the near future.

It had been stressful to walk to that door even though she knew exactly where she stood. Even now, she could feel her heartbeat accelerate. She had held on to her anger, at their entitlement, at the fact that they were allowed to treat her that way—up to a certain point. They would do the same to a patient who went to the clinic for a medically necessary procedure, she knew. Anger was better than the alternative. This wasn't about her though.

Did Wendy have anything to hold on to as she walked past the shouts? Anger? Her husband's support from afar, or knowing that she was going to leave him that day? She wiped a hand over her face, willing herself to focus.

Back to Ashley. The only car registered in Danes's name stood in the parking lot. Had someone picked him up? That meant one bad news on top of the other. He could be more organized than they'd thought. There could be more girls.

Flipping houses was once again sounding more attractive by the minute, until she took a look around her, taking in the mess she hadn't been able to deal with yet. Well, another ten days or so and she could do some heavy lifting on her own.

Kendra had offered to take a look, not that she could magically get those renovations back on track. Luce wasn't even sure she knew anything about the subject, but she appreciated the offer, so much. Perhaps she should have taken her up on another one too.

It was too late for that.

⁂

Exhaustion had hit her out of the blue. Luce left the papers on the table, turned off the coffeemaker and put the leftover pizza in the fridge. Another quick shower. She didn't bother drying her hair but got under the covers and pulled them up high.

Wendy.

Ashley.

How many others?

She wondered if Ritter was better at detaching, spending the evening with his family. Luce liked her privacy, being by herself, but lately there was a lot on her plate.

Thank God for Kendra.

Luce finally fell asleep, her dreams a disturbing mix of people's faces, shouts, cell phones ringing, but she could never get to them. They led her to the room in Danes's basement where he stood over her with a knife, grinning.

"You should have made different choices, Luce."

"Wow. Okay. No more coffee and pizza before bed." She raked a hand through her slightly damp hair, talking to herself out loud to chase away the remnants of that last nightmare. Luce brushed her fingers over the fabric of her top, assured that it wasn't stained with blood.

"Really?" she directed at her subconscious. "I don't need this."

She got up and went to the kitchen to drink some water, making sure every move was conscious and deliberate. That was better. She wondered if Kendra would object to her staying over more often, because nightmares never seemed to be an issue on those occasions. Luce laughed to herself. Talk about privileged, and selfish. She needed to sort out her own stuff, literally and in a metaphoric sense, not taking up more of her friend's space.

Best laid plans. Assured of her good intentions, she went back to bed and soon fell asleep again, undisturbed until the alarm she'd forgotten to turn off the night before.

"You need to figure out what your priorities are," Kendra commented as she took in the progress with a critical eye. "If the contractor you hired can't do the job, you should look for someone new, not let them string you along anymore."

"Yeah. I just don't have the time."

"Says who?"

"Don't start."

Kendra gave her a long, somewhat amused look that made Luce want to fidget.

"Yes, I know I could take some time off just to get things started, no, I don't want to while these cases are open. Yes, I'm irrationally worried about disappointing the only woman boss I've ever had, because she's cool and I want to be her someday."

"Okay. It's a good thing you're on the right side of the law. You'd make a terrible criminal, confessing it all right away."

"Depends on how skilled the other person is."

For a few glorious seconds, suggestion was in the air, possibilities that could exist if they weren't two workaholics who had decided it would be less complicated to ignore subtle hints between the lines. Especially now. It was a part of the fabric of their relationship. Not to be questioned, not to be addressed either.

"One thing where I disagree with her, and Ritter, they want to go easy on the protesters. I don't know. I think things could get out of hand easily, but at the very least they might know something," Luce directed them back to moderately safer waters as they sat on the couch with their coffees and the tiramisu Kendra had brought.

"It's possible that there's a connection," she agreed. "Being confronted with that kind of reaction, it's rough for the patients, whatever their reason for coming to see us."

She was silent for a few seconds. Luce didn't attempt to help her, so Kendra continued. "We have the security measures, we hope for the best. Sometimes, you wonder when something will happen. It's like that low hum all of the time, though it's been getting louder lately. Obviously."

"Recently? How much louder are we talking?"

"I'm not sure. Around the time of the bomb threat there was definitely a spike, then it went down a little. We're getting the usual stuff in the mail, or email. It might not be related, but Wendy going missing after her appointment, it's bothering me."

"I know you're extremely busy, but do you think you could keep an eye out? For anything out of the ordinary?"

"I'll will," Kendra promised. She set her cup down and leaned back against the couch with a sigh. "Did you check on the guy who sent the bomb threat?"

Luce shuddered, remembering that he had done more than that. "He still has some months to go," she said. "Doesn't look like he reached out to anyone, or vice versa."

"Good."

"I don't know how you do this." Maybe she was in a mood, or maybe she felt like this was a conversation they needed to put behind them. "How are you not angry all the time?" She had asked a variation of that question before. Even after everything they'd seen, separately and together during that case, and now, Kendra gave her the same answer.

"Anger takes a lot of energy. Sure, I get angry too, but all that hate and those slurs? They're not worth my time. I prefer to focus on my family and friends, and when I'm at work, my patients."

Luce listened once again to something that made sense, even though she had chosen a different approach. She was grateful for the calm women in her life. Lieutenant Chomsky. Kendra. She wasn't one of them.

"That glass of wine I have on a weekend?" Kendra continued. "Sometimes I come home and want to drink the whole bottle. You know why I don't do it? They don't get to define me, who I am. I deserve good things in my life. So do my patients, no matter what kind of care they seek, no matter the reason. So do you."

The last part caught Luce off guard, causing an unexpected pang of emotion.

"Thank you. I like staying angry. It's motivating."

"Motivation is good. Don't let it take too much from you." After hesitating for a heartbeat or two, she added, "I'm really sorry I wasn't with you."

"Don't be. I asked you not to come."

"There is that."

"And you're providing me with sweets and all the stern words I needed. Kendra, that's all anyone could do."

Kendra leaned forward to embrace her anyway.

"You don't have to worry about me. I have no regrets. I'm okay. I'll still be mad at ignorant people, and the contractor who's ignoring me, and I'll figure out what happened to Ashley and Wendy."

All of it was true. It still felt good to be able to lean on someone, if only for a little while. She could do better reaching out to the people she cared about—or asking for help, but some things were more urgent than others.

"I know you will." There was not a hint of doubt in Kendra's voice, so, Luce shouldn't have any, either.

Chapter Five

Monday passed without them gaining much additional information. Wendy's friends confirmed that she and Steve had been happy about the pregnancy. Their relationship seemed solid.

Luce had briefly talked to the D.A., realizing that she needed a better angle if she wanted to address the protesters some more. D.A. Troy was skeptical that they had much to contribute.

Luce went back to the traffic cameras they had been able to access and was starting to get cross-eyed when Lieutenant Chomsky left her office and headed to her desk in quick strides.

"Allen, where's Ritter?"

She looked up, realizing only now he wasn't at his desk. "I'm not sure...Coffee break, I think."

"I'll have him take over the Ashley Thompson case for now. You can continue when you come back."

"Where am I going?"

"Crime scene," Chomsky returned grimly. "A couple hiking in Cedar Park found a body. We think it's Wendy Tillis."

Luce could feel the blood drain from her face. This couldn't be. It was too soon. She was supposed to find her, bring her home. Alive.

"It's official?"

"They recognized her from the picture. Homicide is on the scene. They'll work with us to solve this as quickly as possible."

"I'm afraid we don't have that much," Luce admitted. "We haven't found her on any of the cameras yet."

"You'll share what you have, and we'll talk later. Now go."

Chomsky was rarely this curt. Luce could tell that she was just as disturbed by the news. She had mixed feelings about Ritter being in charge of the Thompson investigation as well, but perhaps Kendra was right to point out the work would continue with or without Luce.

She left the station steeling herself for the reality of the horrible turn this case had taken. And it was only Tuesday.

❧

To reach the scene, she had to exit the highway onto a smaller street, and then a dirt road between fields leading up to a forested area. The clearing was already crowded with other vehicles, a squad car, the coroner, and one she didn't recognize. Since she was last, she had to park behind them and walk all the way to the yellow tape.

"Detective Allen, Special Crimes," she told the officer. "They're expecting me." With a nod, he held up the tape for her to duck under, and she got her first look at the body, the sight turning her stomach. Luce took a few shallow breaths, determined not to embarrass herself with the Homicide detective, or detectives. They tended to remember things like that forever. Wendy Tillis bore no obvious wounds except for a small bruise on her forehead. What disturbed Luce more than anything was that she'd been showing around the picture of a smiling woman, about to start a family, who was now dead.

"Lieutenant Chomsky told me she'd send someone—"

Luce spun around, feeling her jaw drop. This was it. None of it could be real. She was having another nightmare.

Judging from the detective's expression, he was just as stunned. Coincidence, or that freaking universe laughing at her again.

"Luce," he said. "I'd say it's nice to see you again, but given the circumstances..."

"Yeah. What are you doing here?" Luce bit her lip, maybe to keep another inappropriate question from coming out. She didn't mean to suggest catching up over a dead body. She had no intention of catching up at all.

"Working. Like you." There was a hint of amusement to Tyler Murphy's tone. Also inappropriate. "I transferred recently. I don't know if you remember, but my parents live in the area."

"Yes, of course. So, what happened here?"

"I was hoping you could help me fill in some of the blanks. There's no house or even a shed within miles."

Luce cast another glance. "I guess we can rule out an accident."

"Not officially yet, but it's hard to imagine how she'd end up in this place accidentally."

"Agreed." She stepped closer, pushing back her own visceral reaction—to the scene, the sight, and the other unwelcome surprise—as she crouched down. Donning latex gloves, Luce lifted one of the woman's wrists, then the other. On the left one, she found the bruising she had expected.

Anger. Motivation. "She was held somewhere. He dumped her here. Any tire tracks? He must have come the same way we did, otherwise he would have driven, or dragged her, all the way through those fields." Luce turned around to find Tyler's gaze pensive.

This wasn't just awkward, it was surreal.

"What? You don't think a woman did this?"

"No. I think you might be a few steps too far ahead, but I think it's likely the evidence will lead us there. We found some tire tracks." He looked around the endless stretches of forest and farmland.

"What about the hikers?"

"A couple of twenty-somethings. They are shell-shocked."

"I can imagine." Luce directed her attention back to Wendy Tillis's body, and the small wound on her forehead. Had she fallen? Had someone chased her? She was wearing the clothes Tillis had described to them, but her shoes were missing, her socks dirty. "Her husband told us they really wanted that baby." She wasn't sure why she'd said it out loud, or now. She didn't need a reminder that Wendy's situation had differed greatly from hers, or that the sign-wielding folks wouldn't believe her grief for the victim, and anger at the person who had violently ended this woman's dreams. She suppressed a curse. "I guess that's where we go next."

"You don't have to come."

She knew him well enough to know he wasn't coddling or patronizing her, but Luce didn't want to give anyone the mere appearance either.

"No, I should be there," she said. "My partner thought we should keep looking at him. Financial troubles, something that might have caused a long-term conflict. I'll text you the address. Your number's still the same?"

"It is," he confirmed.

Luce took out her cell phone, found Ritter's text from the other day and forwarded it, wondering briefly why she hadn't deleted the contact. It wasn't like she'd intended to ever use it again.

"Thanks. I'll see you there?"

"Yeah."

Watching him walk to his car, she stood for a few seconds, suppressing a sigh. She knew what Kendra would say. It was the opposite of what she wanted to do, and regardless, the stakes had gotten infinitely higher.

Whoever had done this, she wanted them to pay. Maybe this could convince D.A. Troy that they needed to speak to the protesters again.

It wasn't the first time that Luce had to tell somebody that their loved one wasn't coming back, that despite their best efforts, there wouldn't be a happy ending.

Not as often as Tyler had, she assumed. They had agreed that he'd take the lead during this conversation, while she would observe. She was still on the fence. The bruising around the wrists, the place where the hikers had found Wendy, it didn't make a lot of sense. Yet, he had admitted to some conflict between them.

If Steve Tillis' devastation wasn't real, he was a damn good actor. He broke down in tears halfway through Luce introducing Tyler to him.

"I'm very sorry, Mr. Tillis," Tyler said. "I know this is hard, but we'll need you to come down to the station with us."

Tillis stared at him for a moment before he nodded. "You're sure it's her?"

"Hikers recognized her from the picture you gave my colleague," Tyler told him. His voice was calm, unwavering.

Luce watched Steve Tillis deflate. He cast a look into the corner where the box with the crib still stood against the wall, shook his head as if trying to deny reality before he wiped a hand over his face.

"I have a few more questions, and I'd appreciate it if you could answer them before we go."

Studying Steve Tillis closely, Luce couldn't find anything but grief.

"We went over all of this multiple times already. I gave my statement."

"I know, and like I said, I'm sorry. This is important. Every little detail matters."

"Nothing matters anymore!" With a speed that surprised both of them, Tillis was on his feet and over by the wall where started kicking the crib repeatedly. "She's gone! They're both gone."

"Mr. Tillis. Please."

"Mr. Tillis, I need you to calm down!" Luce's voice seemed get through to him, though he wouldn't be able to return or donate that crib. Had he ever lost his temper like that with Wendy?

He stared at them as if only now remembering there were still two strangers in the room.

"About those questions, Detectives. What do you want to know?"

"Let's go to the station," Tyler declared. "We'll talk there."

Tillis looked like he wanted to object, but he went to pick up his coat and keys.

Chapter Six

The tension settling in her shoulders was near painful, and it remained until the medical examiner drew back the sheet on the other side of the glass. Tillis stayed calm after his earlier outburst, and he stuck to the same story he had given Luce before.

After he had officially identified Wendy, they went to the interview room with him. Tyler got coffee for everyone before they sat down with Tillis.

Only a few minutes later, Luce's phone rang.

"Excuse me, please." She got up and retreated to a corner to answer. Ritter was on the other end.

"Allen, there's a phone call for you at your desk. Someone from the clinic, he says it's urgent."

"I'll be right there," she said. "Anything new...?" She hadn't seen him since earlier that day, but since they never talked about anything but cases, it had to be clear she meant news about Ashley.

"I'm meeting with an informant later," he said. "They might have something."

"Okay. Keep me posted." Luce ended the call and went back to the table. "Detective Murphy, a moment? It won't be long." The last part was for both men. Tillis didn't react at all. He didn't seem to care one way or another.

"Could you wrap up here?" she asked Tyler once they were outside the room.

"No problem. Anything I should know?"

For a heartbeat, this question could have multiple implications.

"I'll let you know if that's the case. I'm not sure yet."

"Okay."

"Thank you, Tyler."

"No problem."

He went back into the room with Tillis, and Luce headed to her desk to answer her phone.

"This is Detective Allen. How can I help you?"

"My name is Marcus Nelson."

His name didn't ring a bell. Luce waited.

"I'm an escort for the Women's Health Center. You know, make sure patients get in there safely."

She knew. He hadn't been working that day though.

"I saw Mrs. Tillis. We exchanged a few words only, but she got into a discussion with some of the protesters. The regulars."

Luce sat up straighter. "I'd appreciate it if you came in, so we could talk in person."

"I'm at work, but if you're still there after my shift? I saw her picture in the news, and I thought it might be important. You're still looking for her, right?"

Luce saw no reason to tell him over the phone that the search had come to an abrupt end.

"You said 'regulars.' Do you have any names?"

"Maggie Rowland, comes with her kid all the time. You might have heard about that candidate for state senate, Jared Hyde. Zach Peters always brings a gun, and there's his buddy Phil. I don't have a last name."

"That's very good. Mr. Nelson, when can you be here?"

"Would around seven be okay?"

"I'll be here," she promised.

Before Luce went back, she did a quick search on the names Nelson had given her. Zach Peters didn't just have an interesting online profile: He also had been accused of domestic violence by a former girlfriend, though the charges had been dropped. The kind of person who would act first, ask questions later?

Maggie Rowland, too, had an easily traceable online footprint, often stirring up discussions, using an inflammatory tone, then claiming harassment when her statements were questioned or debunked. Her daughter was in each of her profile pictures.

Jared Hyde produced by far the most results. He, too, had been accused of domestic violence, but what was equally alarming, he was beating the centrist incumbent in the polls. His positions where everything Luce had expected from a far-right candidate.

She went over some of her notes from a couple of days before, finding what she was looking for: Philip Jameson, the man with the sign she'd talked to in front of the clinic. He had reluctantly given her his information but not revealed anything about the rest of the group. Maggie Rowland, Jared Hyde, Zach Peters.

It was a start.

"There you are," Tyler spoke behind her, startling her. "I don't know about you, but I could use a coffee. Come on. Since I'm the new one here, it's on me."

Luce couldn't find any quick and good reason to say no, so she got up to follow him.

"Thanks."

They had things to talk about after all.

"You first," she said. Instead of going to the break room, they had retreated to a quiet café at the end of the block. Coffee was always a good idea. This...Luce reminded herself she had no reason to feel wistful, about anything. Nothing was anyone's fault. There was always a small probability that contraception could fail.

"Story remains solid, the alibi holds. I believe he has no idea how his wife ended up dead in that field."

"I agree. The clinic had a bomb threat last year, and they get threats on a regular basis. They see a woman go in there, they don't ask why."

"You have someone in particular on your mind?"

"I don't know yet, but the call earlier was from a witness who will come in later. He gave me some names of people I'd really like to talk to."

It was a relief that they could be professional like this—then again, they had never imagined a future together. It shouldn't be a surprise.

"You've been looking at any possibilities unrelated to the clinic?"

"We've been trying to trace her steps." Why did she feel like she had to defend their strategy? Chomsky and Ritter didn't have any objections. "The first time her husband doesn't accompany her, she disappears, turns up dead. The witness saw a group of protesters harassing her. One of them told me she was hysterical. That seems...relevant?"

"I'm not saying it isn't."

They fell silent. Luce wished they had stayed at a station instead of coming here. Even with the shop talk, the setting felt too intimate.

"How have you been?" he asked.

A somewhat loaded question. Luce suppressed the urge to groan, or worse, laugh. It wasn't just one thing. It never was.

Perhaps her visit to her cousin Jill, when she and Tyler had last seen each other, was too much of a reminder of how she didn't have a lot of friends and should connect with family more often. She wasn't close with anyone at work either.

Kendra was the only true constant, and Luce had only known her for about a year. While she valued their friendship more than anything, she was also terrified of doing something to lose it. Catch 22.

"Good. Busy," she said. "Of course I haven't changed work-places twice in the past year. That can't have been easy."

"It's been welcome," Tyler returned with a shrug. "The first time it was because our unit was merged with Homicide, which was part politics, part a lucky coincidence. It helped me when I asked for the transfer."

"I'm glad it worked out for you."

"Yeah. Look, I meant to call you..."

"Don't," she cut in, eager to keep the conversation from veering off into less professional territory. "I didn't expect it." Luce could tell it wasn't what he wanted to hear, but she wasn't going to lie for the comfort of either one of them. Clarity was better than anything, wasn't it?

"Just in case, because we left things somewhat unfinished. I'm sorry about that, but I had a lot on my plate. My dad's health is deteriorating, and my mom needs help. That's part of the reason why I wanted to come here."

"You don't have to apologize. I'm sorry about your dad."

She was, even though meeting the parents had never been part of the plan either.

"Thank you." Tyler's uncomfortable gaze told her that there was more. "I've been seeing Susan," he said.

"That is...good for you." Fantastic was what she'd really wanted to say. A relief. Luce knew that he'd been divorced from his ex-wife for a few years. This news wasn't as hard to take as he might think. In fact, it made her decision much clearer and easier. "Seems like things are coming together."

They would, for her, too. But they had work to do first. Meanwhile, she wasn't going to spring something on him that would complicate every aspect of said work, and their private lives. It wasn't the coward's way out. In fact, it was the right thing to do.

"I hope so," he said. "Now tell me more about that witness. Something tells me we can't be too careful with these people."

"A woman is dead," she returned, bristling. "If any of them hinders the investigation, or becomes part of it, we'll do what's necessary."

"Of course. Perhaps we should catch up with the D.A., see what she thinks."

Luce wasn't looking forward to the last part, though she knew they couldn't avoid it. She hoped that Nelson's statement would convince Troy that Luce was right to keep the focus on the protesters. At least she had Tyler in her corner now.

⁂

Not only did Luce catch D.A. Liz Troy still in her office, but the woman also expressed interest in observing the witness's interview.

"I wanted to hear from you on your progress anyway. We can get started right after your interview."

That came as a surprise to Luce, but if it meant they could move forward with her plans, she'd take it.

"Sure, that works for me."

When she came to work earlier that morning, Luce had hoped she'd be able to leave at a decent time. This wasn't going to happen now. She could take some time once they had found

Wendy's murderer. The turn this story had taken still had her rattled, a stern reminder that her own problems were quite relative in comparison.

She didn't feel guilty. If there was any emotion she was wrestling with it was the constant confrontation with how she'd felt walking those few steps, on the receiving end of the threats and slurs. She didn't scare easily, but that experience sure had put things into perspective. With the realization that there was no way to stop them, legally or with reason, came a sense of helplessness, and she'd hated it. While the physical symptom had abated, that sense hadn't entirely left her.

Ritter had already gone home, Chomsky was about to leave. Fortunately, Marcus Nelson came in early. Her first call went to Tyler.

"I'll be right there," he promised.

"D.A. Troy wants a briefing later. She'll be watching as well."

"You don't sound pleased about it."

Luce imagined he would find out soon enough why she had her reservations about the D.A.

"I'll call her, and once she's here, we can get started?"

"No problem," he returned.

She went to get Marcus Nelson from the waiting area.

"Mr. Nelson, thank you for coming."

"Is it true?" he asked when Luce led him to the interview room. "She's dead?"

Luce suppressed a curse though she hadn't expected it would take much longer for the news to break.

"I'm afraid so. Mr. Nelson, could you wait here for a moment? I'll be right back with you."

"Of course."

She had just gone back to the observation area when Tyler arrived with Troy. He held the door open for her, earning a smile in response. Luce suppressed a sigh.

"Let's do this." If her tone was a bit curt, the D.A. didn't seem to notice.

Inside the room, Nelson waited until Luce had sat down.

"It's really horrible that people feel this entitled to their hate."

"Why do you say that? Did you see anyone threaten her? The names you mentioned?"

"They sure threatened her, but wait...You're saying she was murdered?"

"We don't know for sure yet." No other explanation made sense, but Luce didn't want to share this with him, especially when they were still waiting on the medical examiner's report.

"Wow. What I meant was, it's horrible to die just after being treated that way, but this is even worse. I mean we know there's been violence, but I thought you were looking at them as witnesses."

"You say they were the most vocal?"

"Rowland, yes. I think Hyde uses this as a photo op for his campaign, mostly. What scares me more are the quiet ones like Peters, parading up and down with his gun. He's trying to, I don't know, send a message."

"What kind of message?"

"That there will be consequences? Damn. Someone told me about the bomb threat, but that was a while ago. The guy was caught, wasn't he?" He shook his head, obviously struggling. Luce took a guess.

"I understand that some of the protesters come regularly, but how do you know their names?"

"One of the staff knew Maggie because she has a kid in the same school. Some come from out of town, but others are local...I went to high school with Zach Peters. He doesn't speak to me, but I recognized him. You know that Hyde is running for state senate. Would be a shame if he got elected."

Luce stopped herself short of agreeing with him, though she did after what she'd read on Hyde.

"Have you known Mr. Peters to be violent?" She remembered the accusation, the charges that were dropped.

"We weren't friends or anything, but I remember his parents were extremely strict. I'm sorry I can't tell you anything about recent years."

"That's all right. So, what exactly happened with Wendy Tillis?"

"They crowded her near the door, telling her she could still change her mind," he remembered. "Afterwards, I tried to get her out quickly, but she got in their faces, yelled back at them that whatever she did, it was none of their business."

Luce had entertained doing this, for a split-second, but instead she'd walked past, her shoulders hunched.

"Did anyone touch her? Did she get physical?"

"I was able to intervene before it came to that and convince her to leave. I walked her to her car and waited until she left. That's all I can tell you. I think Zach was laughing at her, at me, I don't know. Then another patient arrived and...You can imagine."

"Do you have any idea where she might have gone after her appointment?"

He lifted his shoulders. "None whatsoever. I made sure she got into the car, and she left. I didn't even think much of it until I saw her picture on the news. I called you right away."

"You did the right thing. Thank you, Mr. Nelson."

This was hardly an occasion to feel hopeful, but she thought that Nelson's statement might convince both Tyler and Troy that they had an angle worth considering.

What scares me more are the quiet ones like Peters.

She'd bet that all of them had something to add to the bigger picture.

Chapter Seven

After Luce had walked Marcus Nelson out, she, Tyler and D.A. Troy settled in the briefing room.

"Okay, tell me, Detective, did you learn anything new? Anything that will help your case?"

The D.A.'s tone was pleasant enough, though Luce realized she wasn't fully convinced.

"I want to talk to each of them. They were the last ones to see Wendy Tillis alive, with the exception of the killer. Maybe. You heard what Mr. Nelson said. They were harassing her."

"That's his version. Come on, Detective, you know that's thin at best. What I heard was someone eager to place the blame. Did you consider that he might have something to hide as well? It doesn't have to be that way, but you better be prepared for all possibilities if you want to haul in a candidate for state senate."

D.A. Troy had a point, Luce had to admit it.

"I'm not hauling in anyone yet. I'll ask them to come down here and talk. Besides, Nelson is not the one with a history of domestic violence."

"Didn't you say the charges were dropped?"

"Yes, but..." She cast a frustrated look at Tyler who was being no help. "We have to be thorough. They might remember something that could help us. If they are at all serious about what they say they stand for, they should want the murderer of a pregnant woman to be caught, don't you think?"

Concern for women certainly wasn't at the heart of the contemptuous hostile behavior they showed towards patients, but she had to make a point. Rule them out or find a likely suspect. Troy's hesitation irritated her. The D.A. didn't make much of an attempt to hide that the feeling was mutual.

"I get what you're saying, but you can't move too fast. Whatever you may think about them, they had a right to be there and express their views. I'm not a fan of Hyde if you must know, but it's a constitutional right."

"And I'm not debating that. What about Wendy Tillis's right to raise a family with her husband?"

"Don't try to twist my words, Detective. I want that person caught just as much as you do. I think you might have to take a look at your own biases."

An awkward pause followed her suggestion, and since Luce wasn't willing to help her out, Tyler spoke.

"D.A. Troy, why don't we schedule those interviews, see what comes up? If we get a hit on the traffic cams, we go from there. We aren't ruling out anything or anyone at this point."

Liz Troy's demeanor changed when she turned to him and gave him a cordial smile.

"That sounds reasonable to me. Thank you both. I'll check in with you tomorrow. Have a good evening. I can see myself out."

After a round of handshakes, she left, and Luce sank back into her chair.

"I said the same thing," she said incredulously.

"I heard you. I also heard that D.A. Troy likes her cases airtight, so all of this is a bit early. I see her point too."

Luce wasn't going to get into a dispute about how the D.A., like many people, was simply more inclined to listen to the same point coming from a man. Tyler wasn't the type to get defensive about this kind of thing, but exhaustion had seeped into her body far too much for that conversation.

She'd have her hands full proving to Troy that she wasn't fishing based on her "biases."

When a woman went missing from a doctor's appointment, men who brought guns and a misogynist platform to express their views were worth looking at.

"I'll make the calls tomorrow and try to get this over with as soon as possible. We can go over the footage from the traffic cams, and the ME should have some more for us."

"Sounds good."

Tyler cast a look at his watch.

"Would you like to grab a bite to eat? Since my apartment wasn't ready when I moved here, I'm still at the hotel, and they have a pretty decent restaurant."

"No, thanks. I need to head home." She caught the hint of disappointment in his expression. Didn't he say earlier he was seeing his ex-wife? Luce was more irritated with herself because she barely stopped before giving him a more detailed explanation. Difficult case, long days, need to get some sleep.

He didn't need to know all of that.

"Another time, then. Good night."

"Good night. See you tomorrow."

She wasn't going to commit to anything. Luce wondered how often Chomsky would want to borrow a Homicide detective. She hoped this would remain an exception.

Luce had good intentions about checking in with the people she cared about. She had promised to call her cousin Jill more often, and she couldn't wait to spend some time with Kendra—all of it would have to wait. Whether she liked it or not, she needed some rest. She couldn't afford any mistakes with those next steps.

At home, she prepared a quick and simple spaghetti recipe, then settled in the living room with a coffee and the cream puff she'd bought on the way home. Caffeine and sweets would go a long way to carry her through this somewhat complicated episode of her life, D.A. Troy being the person who was making it most complicated so far.

Troy was in for the long haul, looking to build a foundation to run for office sometime in the future. Luce wondered if she harbored any biases against the other woman.

Like Kendra, like herself, Troy was confronted with the inevitable misogyny against women in positions of power. Unlike Luce or Kendra, she came from a rich family, well known in law enforcement and political circles that didn't make their conservative leanings a secret.

It didn't have to be a problem. However, it was something Luce had to keep in mind when dealing with her.

She halted her internet research when she nearly fell asleep on the couch, the tablet about to slip from her fingers.

Troy was right in one thing—Luce didn't appreciate women supporting a platform that was too intrusive when it came to other people's lives and decisions. For the sake of providing justice for Wendy Tillis, they'd stay polite with each other.

She could do polite, with Troy, and with Tyler, in order to get the job done.

Luce admitted to herself that he might be one of the reasons why she was stalling both Jill and Kendra.

Jill had certainly picked up something during Luce's visit. She loved Kendra for being kind and insightful, but she might ask questions that Luce didn't want to address. A couple of weeks, and everything would be back to normal.

Maggie Rowland claimed she couldn't come to the station because she didn't have a babysitter for her youngest children, but Luce could go see her sometime in the afternoon.

She rolled her eyes at the phone. Rowland didn't seem to have any trouble finding someone to care for those children when she went to wield signs at the Women's Health Center on most mornings. At least she sounded genuinely disturbed by the news of Wendy's death.

"I don't think I can help you much, but by all means, come by later. This is horrible."

That was at least something they could agree on.

Philip Jameson picked up right away. He wasn't busy.

"Should I bring my lawyer?" he asked.

"That won't be necessary. You aren't being arrested or charged with anything. All we want is to confirm what you said at the clinic the other day."

"That won't be a problem. I'll be right there."

Next, she got Zach Peters' mother on the phone. "The police? This must be a mistake. My son didn't do anything wrong!"

She needed more coffee, Luce mused.

"Could you please get Mr. Peters?"

"I don't know, he might still be asleep. He's been working nights." Her tone sounded both whiny and accusatory. Biases. Right. As irritating as this was, Luce reminded herself that Mrs. Peters senior might have faced a lifetime of expectations to coddle men like her son.

Was this an excuse, when others managed to break the cycle? It wasn't up to her to pass judgment. She could have an opinion, nonetheless. Luce heard some rustling on the other end, hushed voices, then a male voice asked, "What do you want?"

"Mr. Peters, this is Detective Luce Allen. We'd like to talk to you with regards to an ongoing investigation."

"I haven't done anything. Show me a warrant or leave me alone—"

"Mr. Peters, please wait. We've been talking to Mr. Jameson, and we think you might be able to help us. Your contribution would be much appreciated."

"Is this about the woman who died? Yeah, maybe we should talk. Probably one of those quacks that got her killed."

Luce bit her lip. As long as she got him here, she could keep her own emotions at bay. Right?

"Like I said, we'd prefer to talk to you at the station. Any time today would be good, the sooner the better."

"I can be there in an hour."

"That works. Thank you, Mr. Peters."

He hung up on her.

Luce had saved Hyde's office for last, and the moment a woman picked up on the other end, sounding like she was barely legal, she remembered why.

"I'm sorry, but Mr. Hyde can't come to the phone right now. Would you like to leave a message, Detective?"

She considered leaving her number. Luce doubted it would do anything. "No thank you, I'll call you back."

"As you wish. Have a good day, Detective!" she sing-songed.

"That's yet to be determined," Luce muttered.

Tyler looked up from his screen, studying her with a pensive gaze.

"What?"

"Let me try something." He leaned over to snatch the piece of paper she'd used for the numbers and dialed. "Hi, Ms. Grimm. This is Detective Murphy, Homicide. It's important that I speak to Mr. Hyde. No, I'm afraid it can't wait. Thank you, Ms. Grimm."

Luce refrained from rolling her eyes at him. He was probably aware of her impulse, giving her a smug smile.

"Mr Hyde, good morning. As I've told Ms. Grimm, I need to clarify a few things with regard to an ongoing investigation. You're of course welcome to invite your attorney, but I can assure you, you're not accused of anything. The sooner you can be here, the sooner we can clear this up. Thank you so much. We'll be waiting for you."

Luce leaned back in her chair and linked her hands behind her head. "I'm impressed."

"The perks of privilege." He shrugged. "The important thing is that we get those done ASAP."

Luce remembered some of the conversations they'd had at the conference where they first met, and then during her visit to Jill's where her cousin had introduced some of her friends. She liked that he acknowledged those dynamics. She was beyond relieved that they could move on from a couple of brief coincidental encounters to working fairly well as a team.

"Anything on those traffic cams?"

"Nothing. Let's hope we'll have more luck with your angle."

An hour later, that was yet to be determined. Despite his promises, Jameson was a no show, and he didn't answer his phone. Luce decided they would make a detour later this afternoon after meeting with Maggie Rowland.

That left Zach Peters and Jared Hyde, the candidate for Councilman who had written extensively on his perceived immorality of unmarried women, abortion, and a multitude of other subjects.

Before either one of them arrived, Luce received a call from the medical examiner.

"I'm afraid we have some inconclusive findings," he warned her. "We still have to wait for the full tox screen, but for one, we found a sedative in her blood."

Unlikely that she had taken it. "She was drugged?"

"The concentration, along with the ligature marks, would indicate it. No signs of violence other then the small wound on the forehead...She could have fallen and hit her head."

"How? You said it's pretty clear that she was held somewhere."

Luce remembered that the ground had been hard, though that would have to be a lot of bad luck.

"I didn't say that, Detective. It looks like it, but there are some inconsistencies. Her last meal was some sort of stew. She died the next night, likely from exposure. I told you some of it was inconclusive."

"You did. Anything else?"

This was bad news. How did Wendy Tillis get from the place her kidnapper took her to, to that field? And if her death happened during her escape, what did that mean for his motive? The pieces didn't come together yet, though Luce was sure that when they did, the picture would be sinister.

She imagined Wendy running as fast as she could, with no shoes, her kidnapper possibly pursuing her.

"Time of death approximately between 2:00 and 5:00 a.m. I'll get back to you when we have the results of the full tox screen."

"Yes, thank you."

When she hung up the phone, it rang almost immediately, the officer at the front desk calling to notify her that Jared Hyde had arrived.

"Come on," she said to Tyler. "I'll tell you on the way."

Chapter Eight

Jared Hyde was forty-two, according to his website. Luce thought he looked older, but it might be his policy positions that gave her that impression.

"Detective Allen, how can I help you?"

He sat, leaning back in his chair, comfortable, smiling.

Luce laid the picture of Wendy Tillis in front of him.

"Do you remember her?"

"Should I?"

He took a closer look "The woman who was found dead? What a tragedy for her husband, losing both mother and child."

"You ever spoke to her?"

"I speak to a lot of people, Detective. I'm afraid I can't remember them all."

So, he wanted to play it that way.

"According to a witness, you had an extended hostile interaction with her at the Women's Health Center. Care to explain?" She kept her voice low and polite, but Luce could tell he had caught her subtle reproach, his eyes narrowing.

"That's an opinionated way to put it. We were trying to keep her from making a mistake she would regret for the rest of her life, don't you agree?"

His attitude was nothing new or original. Luce tried to summon Kendra's calm, *not worth my time. Focus.* She found it interesting that he had already given up on denying he knew Wendy.

"But things didn't work out that way. Wendy Tillis is dead. Besides, it doesn't matter what I think. She went to the clinic for prenatal care. It seems to me you're the opinionated one if you didn't even care to ask."

Behind her, Ritter cleared his throat.

Hyde shrugged, unfazed by her words. "It's better to be safe than sorry. We want to save as many as we can. If we happen to offend someone's...sensibilities, so be it."

"Tell me about the interaction you had."

"Sure. We tried to engage her, but she wouldn't listen, got quite vulgar."

"That bothers you? A woman using bad language?" Talk about sensibilities.

He kept the smile in place. "I don't like it, if you must know, but there's not much I can do about it, is there? Detective...Allen, is it? I was told that this was important. I'm sorry about Mrs. Tillis, but if that's all you need, I'm afraid we'll have to end this conversation. As a police officer, you must understand wanting to protect all lives?"

Luce refrained from saying out loud what sprang to mind, that according to his platform, he mostly cared about the lives of rich white men. She understood it wouldn't be productive.

"What exactly did she say to you?"

"If that so-called witness exists, you must already know? Forced birther, anti-choice, all those clever words they use. I would have never known that she was actually happy to be expecting. I admit it got a little heated. That was not the plan, but she wouldn't stop yelling. Sad," he ended his statement, shaking his head.

Luce sat back, amazed at how she could find all of it completely predictable, but still felt stunned at his brazenness to place the blame on a dead woman.

"And how did you react?"

"I begged her not to go back. She threw a few more curse words at me and the others, and left with that guy, that escort. Maybe you should ask him—he doesn't seem to have a problem with murdering babies."

Calm. Focus. Nothing she'd say or do would change the man's mind. It wouldn't make a difference for Wendy. Or herself.

"That's a heavy accusation."

"Oh, come on, you can do better. I'd like to help, but that was the only time I saw Mrs. Tillis, and I don't know what happened to her afterwards. She was hysterical, so maybe she did run away. Who knows? But maybe this can be a chance for all of us. I'm planning to serve my community too. It means that one of the first things we'll do is to shut them down for good."

"How will that serve anyone?" She couldn't help it.

"You heard me, Detective. It's sad that Wendy and her child had to die, and I hope you'll find the person who did it. But I don't see you bringing in those doctors for what they do. Think about it. Probably you should."

"We don't bring in people randomly. We follow the law." He could make of that what he wanted to. "Thank you for your time, Mr. Hyde. It's been most enlightening."

Her stomach did a somersault at the idea that sometime soon, the law could look different even here. What would she do then?

"You're welcome, Detective Allen." He stood, looking her up and down in a way that was highly inappropriate for the setting. Or any setting. "Good luck."

If he thought she'd return the wish, he was mistaken.

"He's unpleasant," Tyler commented after Hyde had left. "I'll give you that. But I don't think he knows anything. That means the others probably don't either..." He held up a hand. "I'm not saying it's a done deal yet, but we should be ready to shift gears."

"I hear you. I'd still like to check a few things."

"Sure. We'll go and pay Rowland and Jameson a visit after a quick lunch?"

Luce wasn't sure how she felt about those regular meals together, but she couldn't deny it would be more efficient. "I guess that works. I haven't heard from D.A. Troy, so I assume she's waiting to hear from us."

At her desk, she went back to her earlier search on Jared Hyde. She was inclined to agree with Tyler, but she didn't want any loose ends either. A search for donations yielded the expected results. One interesting aspect: A prominent group had withdrawn their support over what they understood as a call for violence. Hyde was more popular than anyone with his positions should be, but his campaign apparently had some financial issues.

She had no idea yet how this could matter. Luce wasn't ready to admit that she might be on the wrong track. The next twenty-four hours would show whether or not she was.

Since it was still early in the afternoon, they decided to see Jameson first. He didn't apologize about standing them up, and he gave them the same tired lines. At that point, Luce was willing to acknowledge that this might be a fishing expedition.

Maggie Rowland appeared frantic and overwhelmed when she opened the door to them. In addition to the girl she'd dragged to the Women's Health Center, she had a boy who was doing elementary school homework at the kitchen table, and another boy and girl under the age of five.

"What do you want to know?" she asked, crossing her arms over her chest in a defensive stance. "I haven't broken any laws. We have a permit, if you want to see it."

"I believe you," Luce said. She had to raise her voice over the loud play of the youngest kids. Tyler wasn't much help, observing the scene with a mix of amusement and preoccupation. "You go to the Women's Health Center often, then, if you filed for the permit."

"Yes, of course. It's important to stand up for the unborn. You won't do it."

Here we go. Luce suppressed a sigh.

"A witness told us you and some others were harassing Wendy Tillis on the day she went missing."

Rowland shook her head with the patient expression someone would extend to a highly naïve person, or a child.

"They said that? They're lying. I am so sorry for Mr. Tillis. This should have never happened, but she was attacking us and our views before that man pulled her away."

"You mean, physically?"

"No. I don't know. I was worried. Sometimes these things can get out of hand. She got very nasty."

"Did you see her again after that morning? Or where she went?"

"No. We are pretty busy there. We can't go after every lost cause, something you might understand, Detective. I saw you there."

For a heartbeat, Luce froze. Tyler didn't seem to have picked up on the possible implications. Maggie Rowland's stubborn gaze told her she had brought up the subject at this particular moment on purpose.

"The doctors get death threats," she said. "We care about their lives too, as should you."

"I guess we have different priorities. I never saw Mrs. Tillis except that morning. She was screaming at Mr. Hyde until the escort convinced her to go. We stay within the perimeter. I don't know, someone else might have gone after her to take a picture of her license plate or home."

Her casual tone, as she related the possibilities, sent a chill down Luce's spine.

"You do that, follow people home, take pictures?"

Tyler's tone, pleasant and cordial until now, had taken on a sharp edge. It was comforting. Luce often felt like she was shouting into a void, except when she was with Kendra. Her friend knew firsthand how, in her line of work, ideology and actions posed a threat to her, and her colleagues and patients.

It wasn't so much that everyone agreed with Hyde or Rowland, but too many were fine with looking the other way.

"I don't," Maggie said with a shrug. "I don't blame the ones who do it either. It's not a fair fight, not yet."

"You got any names?"

"I'm sure Mr. Hyde doesn't have the time, but a couple of the other regulars? I see them on and off, but not all of them are with the Defenders of Life," she explained. "You can look us up online if you're interested in protecting the truly vulnerable."

"Do you have names for any of those regulars?"

"Not really."

Her hesitation hadn't gone unnoticed.

"Mrs. Rowland, I understand you don't want to get anyone into trouble. From what I hear, you and your friends have everything in order. You have the right to express your views." She might be gritting her teeth a little, but so far, this was the truth. "If someone among you is looking to pick a fight, or cross

62

boundaries, I don't believe that's you. But you might want to be careful going out on a limb for them."

"I really don't know the name," Maggie said. "Guy with a beard, comes with a rifle. He bought ice cream for the kids one time."

"He takes pictures of the license plates?"

"I heard someone talk about that one time. That's all."

"Is that him?"

She cast a quick glance at the picture Luce showed her.

"Could be. I'm not sure."

"Okay, Mrs. Rowland, thank you for your time. Please don't hesitate to call if you remember anything else."

Rowland took the card from Tyler, her smile genuine. Luce suppressed a sigh.

"Thank you," she said. "We can see ourselves out."

Back in the car, Tyler was suspiciously silent. She was used to this from Ritter, but at the moment, it worried her.

"That sounded like Zach Peters."

She got a non-committal sound in reaction.

"Come on, Jameson, Rowland, Hyde and Peters. One of them follows patients home."

"So that's where you decide to put your faith in Mrs. Rowland?"

He spoke without sarcasm, just mild curiosity, but the words still hit home.

"It has nothing to do with faith, and you know it. She wants to keep doing what she's doing. They might like to toss around the word murder, but they can't be associated with a real murderer. I think she was telling the truth."

"Guy with a beard and a gun. That's vague, and you heard her. She wasn't sure."

"Well, then it's a good thing he's still on our list. Let's wake him up early tomorrow morning..." Reading his expression easily, she added, "You are not convinced."

"I think it's a shame that they won't leave people alone, when abortions are only a small percentage of what they do at that clinic," he said.

Luce refrained from the impulse to tell him that no matter the percentage, it wouldn't be any of Rowland's business. Or Peters'. She needed someone in her corner for her plan to haul Peters out of bed quite literally.

"But?"

"But I'm not sure if there's any connection to our case. Do they talk a big game, sure."

"That bomb threat last year was a whole lot more than talk."

"I agree, but abduction? That's more personal. I want to talk some more to Steve, Wendy's friends. An angry ex might be the more logical explanation."

"I looked into that in the beginning." She was trying hard not to sound defensive. "Steve and Wendy met in college. She never mentioned an abusive ex."

Luce knew what Tyler was going to say.

"Doesn't mean he doesn't exist."

"Doesn't mean Zach Peters didn't follow her home. Husband was at work. Wendy wasn't showing that much, so Zach doesn't believe she didn't go to the clinic for an abortion and decides to punish her?"

"It's a possibility," he admitted.

"Thank you." What if she had missed anything? No. Luce went over the conversations with Steve Tillis in her head, her and Ritter's preliminary reports. They had covered all the bases.

She had to be one hundred percent certain, because she still had to convince Chomsky and Troy that this continued to be a valid line of investigation.

No one would be happier to be done with it than Luce, but her instincts told her they had to keep looking.

She was ready to call it a day, preparation to pick up Peters tomorrow morning in place, when Chomsky called her into her office. The woman seldom raised her voice, still, her tone made Luce cringe and hesitate for a heartbeat.

"You need some backup in there?" Tyler asked, half-serious.

"Thanks, but no."

"Please, close the door," Chomsky said when Luce walked inside. "Can you explain this?"

She showed Luce the headline of a newspaper's website. Jared Hyde sounding off on being interviewed as a possible witness wasn't worth any headache, in Luce's opinion.

"He was polite earlier, but I guess it's not a surprise that he's trying to use this to create some media buzz. He's a caricature even to some in his own circles. It will have blown over by tomorrow."

"You're surprisingly cavalier about this. He's accusing the police department of having an agenda against the entire movement."

"He's also accusing doctors who do their jobs and always put their patients first, of murder."

"Yes, I know. I'm not particularly worried about Mr. Hyde, but either way, we can't be seen as being political." She held up a hand. "I know what you want to say, Detective, and I agree with you. But these are the perimeters we work within. Imagine if the roles were reversed."

"But they aren't." *They never are.* She straightened her shoulders. "I hear what you're saying. I still think we need to see this through to find Wendy Tillis's murderer."

"There are still no other leads?"

"We are talking to one Zach Peters tomorrow who seems to have the habit of following patients, taking pictures of them."

"Wrap it up soon. Regardless of what we believe, all this attention isn't making those doctors' work any easier."

"Yes, Ma'am. Is that all?"

"For now. Let me know when Peters is here."

Luce nodded and left the office. She said a quick goodbye to Tyler, not leaving any room for more small talk, before she headed to her car and sat inside. A few calming breaths. It was something Kendra did. Thinking of her, Luce was overcome with longing for her warmth and words, something that had both intrigued and confused her for some time now. Mostly the former, though.

Not that Kendra was interested in dating her—they had been friends for too long for it to still be an option.

If it had been...Her thoughts rarely went further than that. She had a job to do, a few issues to wrestle with. Once Kendra started dating someone new, it would likely clear up her own confusion in a heartbeat.

Chapter Nine

F ighting the impulse to call it a day and simply order in, Luce stopped at a supermarket to buy some fresh ingredients, her mind still on Peters.

Tomatoes and herbs.

She shook her head at the thought of Maggie Rowland and the other parents letting him buy treats for their kids, the silent guy with the rifle.

Next, she put fresh pasta and mozzarella in her cart.

Peters might have been following patients.

Wendy?

It was personal, Tyler had suggested.

Perhaps one glass of wine with dinner? Luce found a half liter bottle that might not go bad in her fridge.

And Jared Hyde, of course he wouldn't keep his mouth shut after they'd taken less than an hour of his precious time. Time that he could have spent...trolling women, and his opponent on the Internet?

The tiramisu from the dessert aisle wouldn't be as good as Kendra's homemade one, but she didn't have all night.

Luce paid at the cash register, still deep in thought as she carried her purchases to her car and went home.

She nearly cursed when she saw the still unfinished part. She had forgotten to call the contractor, and apparently, they weren't making any moves either. She was tired of living with the construction site, tired of ignorance, of having to accommodate it.

If there was any money left at the end of the renovation saga, she'd finally take a vacation. Italy maybe.

A homemade dinner with a glass of Chianti was a good start.

She was about to make some coffee for her dessert, her wine glass still half full when the phone rang.

"Detective Allen," she answered without thinking.

"That sounds serious." Jill's tone, on the other hand, was cheery. "I hope I'm not interrupting anything. I just wanted to hear how you were."

"I'm good. Busy. As I'm sure you are."

"Always," Jill admitted. "Crimes and pre-school have a way of keeping me that way."

Jill had a daughter, about the same age as one of Maggie Rowland's. Strange to think of the two women in the same sentence.

"I can imagine." Luce remembered that she'd wanted to invite her too, not to wait too long, now that they had reconnected. "I still have plastic tarps and dust all over the place, but I harbor the hope that it will all be done one day. Maybe you and Josie would like to come visit then."

"We totally would." Luce couldn't blame her for sounding a bit surprised. "Isn't there other news too?"

"Like what?"

"Ellie tells me that one of her colleagues transferred to your department. You might be running into him again."

"If you're talking about Murphy, I already have. My boss borrowed him for an investigation."

"That sounds intriguing."

"It's work. Nothing intriguing about kidnapping and murder."

Jill wasn't easily deterred.

"You two got along well when you were here."

"I get along with everyone," Luce joked even though they both knew it wasn't true.

Jill, catching up on the fact that Luce wasn't going to tell her any more details, changed the subject to her latest work. They agreed to talk again soon.

"And please, send me those articles. I'd love to read them."

"Sure. Thanks."

"You're welcome."

Luce went back to her interrupted dinner. As she finished her wine, she thought about when Jill took her to the bar run by her friend's in-laws. She had met Ellie Harding, her wife and their colleagues, Wu, Doss, and Henderson. The latter two had obvious history, though he was there with his wife, and Maria Doss was dating a stunning woman named Valerie Esposito, the A.D.A.

Despite the strained relationship law enforcement had with the press sometimes, Jill was at ease, and they were quite welcoming to strangers. Luce had found herself wistful observing the easy camaraderie between the colleagues, wishing it was something she had here at home.

"And here's Murphy, late as always," Doss commented. "Hey, Tyler. Meet Jill's cousin."

Luce cringed a bit at the memory, thinking it was probably obvious to everyone, including Jill, that they'd already met. And that she had snuck into Jill's house late that night.

She swirled the wine around in her glass. One cocktail. She never drank that much anyway, so she could never blame her decisions, good or bad, on alcohol. Back at the conference—why not?

During a visit that was meant to reconnect with family as Kendra had encouraged her to, Kendra always on her mind, maybe it hadn't been such a good idea, but what was done was done.

The phone rang again, and with a sigh she thought she might never get to that store-bought tiramisu. Luce picked up the phone while taking a plate out of the cabinet.

"I know where you live," the disembodied voice said.

"Who is this?" she asked sharply, not expecting an answer. Luce didn't get any.

She mumbled a swear word and finally opened the box. It was probably time to change her number.

She wasn't going to spend any more time than necessary on Peters. Luce had several items on her work desk she needed to get to. At six-thirty a.m., she wondered if she could get to some of them before they went to pick him up, when the doorbell rang.

Opening the front door to Tyler, she couldn't manage much of a poker face.

"Hey, don't make that face. I know it's early, but you're dressed, and I brought breakfast."

"Then you're welcome." She stepped aside to let him in.

"Happy to hear it. You have a nice—whoa. Home that's in the process of becoming nicer I guess."

"Yeah. I guess I jumped on the open concept bandwagon. It's been long. I might have to change contractors...but you're not here for that," she changed gears. "Let's have that breakfast."

"If you need any help just let me know. I did some projects for our first house back in the day."

"Thanks. I want to go back to the scene later."

If that was too much of an abrupt change of subject, Tyler didn't mention it. Luce suppressed a sigh when he deposited his purchases on the table and took a seat, more than comfortable. Showing up uninvited, albeit with food, wasn't a good sign, especially while he was reconnecting with his ex.

Luce was still happy for him.

"Sure, let's do that," he agreed. "Anything else?"

The coffee was still hot which lifted her spirits some.

"Just some other research I wanted to do, on Hyde…" She knew how to interpret that expression. "He's been getting money from businesses, some churches and organizations like Maggie's, but his campaign is close to broke. Where did all that money go?"

"That might be a question for another unit. I thought your money was on Peters."

"I never said that." Luce didn't take a seat but remained leaning against the counter. Almond and chocolate croissants. Even people who didn't know her very well were aware of her sweet tooth. "Speaking of Peters, depending on how this morning goes, we might have to put a trace on him. If he regularly doxxes patients and employees, we should know."

"Putting someone's address on the Internet is bad, but it's a long way from abduction."

Was it, though?

"But it can lead to it, and there should be some accountability either way."

"No argument from me."

"You think I'll get one from Troy, or do you think you can sway her with your charm? Yeah, forget I said that."

"Too late now," he joked. "Luce, you've got to relax sometime. Troy isn't unreasonable. We want to solve this case, we can't get distracted."

She thought of a response and decided against it. They had a person of interest to pick up.

"You're right. Let's go and wake Zach."

"You've been looking forward to this."

"Kind of."

He laughed. "As much as this case sucks, this is going to be fun."

⟡

"My son works hard. I told you he was doing night shifts!" Peters' mother greeted them with indignation. "What's all this?" she asked, indicating the squad car on the other side of the street. "You're telling me you want to arrest him for saving those babies? Do you *know* the kind of people who go into that place?"

"Ma'am," Tyler interrupted the flow of words. "I'm sorry that we can't always be so accommodating. Mr. Peters isn't under arrest. We just need to confirm something with him, and he's free to follow us in his own car."

"Why would I do that?" Peters arrived behind his mother, wearing jeans and a grey undershirt. "You've been harassing me. I've got nothing to say to you."

"See?" Mrs. Peters' voice held a hint of triumph.

"We want to make sure that what happened to Wendy Tillis won't happen to anyone else, and we think you might be able to help us," Luce said. "If any misunderstandings have happened along the way, the station is the best place to clear them up."

When Peters still stared at her blankly, she added. "You always buy sweets for the kids at the protests? Someone could easily misunderstand that."

"What are you saying?" His mother's voice rose a few notches.

"It's nothing, Mom. Forget about it." He glared at Luce once more. "I'll be right behind you. You better not be messing with me."

"Thank you for your cooperation, Mr. Peters."

She and Tyler went back to her car after a furious Mrs. Peters slammed the door shut.

"That was quicker than expected."

"Fingers crossed for the rest," he mumbled.

Chapter Ten

"Mr. Peters, you aren't a member of the Defenders of Life. Or any other similar organization."

"I don't see why that should matter."

"But you know Maggie Rowland. You bought her daughter ice cream."

"So? It was a hot day. Everyone appreciated it."

Tyler gave her a look that indicated she should speed it up. Given that D.A. Troy was watching on the other side of the glass, Luce agreed with him, even though she would never understand why anyone was comfortable having this guy approach their child.

"Nothing wrong with that. So, you're sort of a freelancer."

"Again, I can't see what difference that would make. We all have the same goal, to stop the killing, any way we can."

"Is that why you bring a gun?"

"Does the trick sometimes. I've never shot anyone, if that's what you meant."

"Did it convince Wendy Tillis?"

"You're wasting your time. Mine too."

"Am I? Did Maggie get that wrong? I thought you went after Wendy. She made you angry, perhaps you thought it was a good idea to put her personal information on the Internet? A picture of her license plate? Her home?" She was raising her voice, but barely.

It did the trick.

"Hey, if that makes you angry, maybe you should think about why. You are all pathetic. Protect and serve, right? You only serve a bunch of killers."

"Whatever you say, Zach. But you made a mistake with Wendy. She wanted to be a mother."

"It's not true," he mumbled.

"Her husband told us, her doctors confirmed it. Why do you think you know better?"

"A hunch," he said with a smug grin, the brief moment of alarm gone.

The phone on the wall rang.

"Excuse me for a moment." *Not a good time, Troy.*

"Allen, I want you two to take a break," Lieutenant Chomsky said on the other end.

"Yes, Ma'am."

"We'll be back in a few minutes," Luce told Peters, trying to keep her frustration out of her tone. She could tell she hadn't entirely succeeded.

They went to the observation area where Chomsky stood with Troy, their expressions unreadable.

"We have a missing teen," Chomsky said without preamble. "Let's go talk in my office before you wrap up."

The news made her stomach churn with apprehension.

"Another? What if Danes—"

"We don't know yet if it's related."

She turned to look at the man behind the glass who appeared far too comfortable for someone in his situation. Luce wasn't sure she was done with him, but she didn't have much of a choice.

"Could I talk to Detective Allen for a moment?"

76

Chomsky looked from Troy to Luce and nodded. "Detective Murphy and I will be in my office."

Troy waited until they were alone in the room, then she said, "I think we can all agree you can let this go now. You're going around in circles, and if I'm not mistaken, your lieutenant is already feeling the pressure."

"Excuse me? My lieutenant is aware that we are doing what's necessary, including ruling out suspects who were seen harassing Wendy Tillis hours before her death."

Tyler might have a point saying that she needed some time to relax, but Luce knew she wasn't going to get it anytime soon. A woman was dead, and someone was responsible. Shouldn't that be everyone's focus?

Troy didn't socialize with the likes of Peters, or maybe even Maggie Rowland, but she wasn't hiding her views either. Neither did her parents, long-time donors to politicians more subtle than Hyde, but united when it came to various subjects. Including this one.

"They're pro-life. So am I. It's not enough reason to go after someone. So, they exchanged some slurs which is unfortunate. You want to arrest everyone who throws a bad word at you? I'm sure that has happened on the job."

Luce should have reminded her that doxxing and stalking someone went beyond a loud and colourful argument, but her patience was waning. She was tired—all of which was an explanation, not an excuse. She knew.

"You don't get it. Why am I not surprised?"

"Excuse me?"

Luce and Kendra had often talked about the phenomenon in general, people in positions of power who considered themselves apolitical on the job. In Luce's opinion, there was no such thing.

"You know what I mean." And yes, perhaps that anger at the world took too much energy sometimes. She had been angry on behalf of others, and herself, including at someone like Troy who'd flat out refuse to acknowledge how her actions made the lives of others harder.

"Do you think I'm stupid?" the D.A. asked, her tone icy and incredulous.

"No, I think you're smart, and that scares me more," Luce answered. "He?" she said with a nod to the man behind the glass. "He'll slip up at some point, hurt someone, maybe even kill, if he hasn't already. He's treading the line, wants the spotlight, and eventually he might go to jail for it. Someone like you, educated, polite, quietly slips into power and brings their prejudice to work. It has happened before. This is why we are where we are right now."

The woman's face reddened. "You know nothing about me, Allen."

"I know you are able to do harm, but you'd never admit it. It's not just about the patients getting yelled at by people who need to mind their damn business. It's about limiting access, endangering someone's livelihood and life, and you think you're acting on behalf of the innocent."

"Allen! That's enough! My office, now!"

"It's about time," D.A. Troy mumbled.

Luce didn't bother with a response but followed Lieutenant Chomsky into her office, her back straight. She didn't regret a thing, least of all speaking truth to questionable power.

She wanted to sleep for a day or two, but Wendy Tillis's murderer was still out there. Joe Danes was still out there.

"Allen, what the hell is wrong with you? I understand getting frustrated with someone like Peters, but D.A. Troy is not your enemy."

Isn't she? She almost asked. Chomsky might have a point, to some extent, Luce reflected. She herself was privileged enough not to have her rights infringed on too much, yet. At least she'd still been able to make that decision, though it would be in question if some people got their way entirely. For some, it already was reality.

"About that missing teen," she said.

"Nice try, Allen. Detective Murphy will get the file started and fill you in later. I'll talk to D.A. Troy and see what I can do so we can stay on track with this investigation, and you'll inform Mr. Peters that he's free to go."

"Lieutenant, with all due respect..."

"That's all, Detective. I suggest you apologize to the D.A. for what you implied."

However, when Luce returned to the interrogation room, Troy had already left. Luce couldn't be more grateful for the temporary reprieve.

She was aware of Tyler studying her. She didn't comment.

"Mr. Peters," she said, forcing a smile. "I will see you out."

As they walked to the front door, she told him, "Thank you for your help. A word of advice: Don't expose anyone's information for a while."

His intense stare turned into smile.

"I have some advice for you. Make sure you know whose side you're on. Don't be on the wrong one. Have a good day."

Luce stood for a few seconds, wondering if he was bluffing.

"Everything okay?" the officer at the front desk asked her.

What a loaded question. "Yep," she said and headed back to her desk. She still wanted to go back to the crime scene before dark.

"Cory Baldwin, fifteen, went missing from a group home. Are you listening to me?" Tyler asked, sounding impatient as he filled her in on the new case.

"Yes, of course. We'll get an Amber Alert out?"

"Already done. Another girl from the house is a witness. They were in town together, she saw Cory being pulled into a car."

Luce tried to get a rein on the chaos on her mind, Troy, Chomsky's warnings, the not-so-subtle threat Peters had made. Anger and resignation. Another teen missing.

"We're going there or—?"

"She's on her way here now. Jesus, Luce."

"No need to bring Him into this."

"This could become serious. Hyde is already having a field day. I understand how you feel about him, but D.A. Troy? She's just doing her job. Suggesting anything else won't make ours easier."

Luce had no desire to discuss any of this with him.

"We should set up in the conference room. I don't want her to be intimidated or hold anything back. Did she say what they were in town for?"

Tyler gave her a quizzical look. "They're teenagers. Shopping? Hanging out at the mall?"

She shrugged, making a mental note to ask. Luce couldn't give a rational reason why this seemed important. She cast a glance at her watch.

"We can still make it back to the scene today, right?"

"I think so."

She couldn't say why this was important either. She just knew it was.

Perhaps she needed to distract herself and the people around her from the fact that she'd almost made a huge mistake. Luce had no problem with atonement, but she was starting to fear that everyone was right, that she might be off her game.

Ashley Thompson should be home right now.

Wendy Tillis should be alive.

She pushed her dire thoughts aside as a uniformed officer came heading their way to inform them that the witness was here to see them.

Chapter Eleven

A woman in her mid-forties introduced herself as Mrs. Meyers. She was accompanying Angelica Rollins who had witnessed what they assumed to be an abduction.

Luce took in the pair, thinking that Meyers appeared to be gentle, trying to comfort the girl. Angelica barely made eye contact, fidgeting before she sat in the chair.

It might be the setting that made her uncomfortable. Luce hadn't made up her mind yet.

"Angelica, thank you for talking to us," she said, keeping her voice low. "I can understand this is hard for you, but can you describe the car or the driver at all?"

"I didn't get much of a look at him...I was so shocked. I was just going into the store for snacks. Cory stayed on the other side of the street, because she was checking out the shop window...When I came back out, I saw him pull her in, and he hit the gas. I think she was too surprised to react." She seemed to remember the actual question. "Older white guy. He had sunglasses on. I'm sorry."

She sounded close to tears.

"That's all right." If the store had a security camera, that footage might help them identify the kidnapper. "Is there anything else you remember? Do you know if someone had approached Cory before, or threatened her?"

Luce knew she was on to something when the girl looked like she was trying to disappear, wrapping her arms around her body as if she wanted to shrink in on herself.

"Detective, this has been a traumatic day for Angelica," Mrs. Meyers reminded her. "I hope you can wrap this up soon."

You and me both.

"I'm sorry. If you can think of anything, or anyone who might have seen something earlier, please let us know right away."

Angelica finally dared to look up and nodded.

"Can you tell me why you were in town today?"

"No reason. Just to hang out."

Luce might be off her game, but she still knew when someone was lying to her face.

"You do that often?"

"Whenever we have the time."

"You're good friends?"

"Detective," Meyers interrupted again. "I don't see why this matters."

"I'd like to speak to Angelica alone for a moment."

"Absolutely not! I'm responsible! What are you insinuating? It's not her fault."

"I'm not saying that. I want to make sure that we know everything that happened today, so we can bring Cory home safely."

A heavy silence hung over the room as the seconds ticked by.

Finally, Angelica spoke, her tone so low Luce had to lean closer to understand her.

"I promised her I wouldn't tell anyone."

"Tell anyone what?" Mrs. Meyers asked. Much to her credit, she showed nothing but concern.

Angelica dropped her gaze to the tabletop. Much as she empathized, Luce had to curb the impulse to tap her fingers. They had to go back to that field.

"She had an appointment at the...Women's Health Center for a procedure. An abortion."

"Angelica." Mrs. Meyers sounded perplexed. "Why didn't she tell anyone?"

"We looked it up, she doesn't have to," Angelica defended herself. "But we didn't know she'd have to wait a couple of days."

"I know this was hard, but you did the right thing telling us. The more we know, the better we can help Cory. When you went to the Women's Health Center, did anyone talk to you outside, anyone who seemed threatening?"

"If you're asking that, you already know," she said, sounding older than her age, and resigned, all of a sudden. "There were people with signs, a few of them yelling at us. Well, we knew about that too, and we didn't talk to anyone."

Her eyes were welling up.

"If I hadn't gone in for that stupid bag of chips, none of this would have happened."

Luce wasn't going to tell her that the man who had targeted Cory Baldwin would have likely tried again. Kidnapping the Health Center's patients. They had to warn everyone. That was more important than getting back to the field. They could still do that tomorrow.

"Do you know who the father is?" Tyler asked.

"Her boyfriend. He's a good guy, he's supporting her...but he had to work today, so she asked me to come."

Another absent partner, a couple, albeit in a highly different situation from the Tillises...but they'd already learned that Jameson, Hyde, Peters, and Rowland didn't do a lot of research. Luce didn't think the mother of four would go as far as actually kidnap someone. Of the rest of them, Peters still looked good to her, but she was also interested in where Hyde spent all that money he got from donors. Or if Jameson had tried to slip under the radar. Was one of them covering for the other?

"One more thing. You remember the name of the doctor she saw?"

"Yes, it was a Dr. Jones. Cory said she was very kind."

This might make things easier and more complicated at the same time.

"All right, Angelica, Mrs. Meyers, thank you for coming. We'll be in touch."

This time, Tyler walked them out while Luce went to get her coat and keys.

She met him in the parking lot, and they took his car.

"You can say it." He too, sounded resigned, making her wonder where he was going with this.

"It was a hunch. I'm not happy about being right. In fact, we don't know for sure yet." The coincidences were adding up though, and all traces led back to one place.

"You think someone is going after patients? Going to their home is bad enough, but..."

"We've been over this. If you're ready to kill someone with a bomb, it's already personal."

"But we have no reason to believe that the two are related."

"No, that guy is still behind bars. That's not the point either. There's more than one dangerous person in the mix, even though Troy doesn't see it. I hope this will wake her up."

"To prove a point?"

"No," she shot back, "to save a girl's life. That's what we're trying to do here if I'm not mistaken. I'll see if Kendra is on duty. I'm sure she can help us."

"All right then."

They made the rest of the drive in silence.

Since it was later in the day, there were fewer protesters. Luce didn't recognize anyone except Maggie Rowland. This time, she didn't have her daughter with her.

She thought about how odd it was to walk the same way...She could have told Tyler. He wasn't the type of person to freak out and place the blame over something that was clearly nobody's fault, on her, but Luce didn't think it would matter one way or the other.

They had never intended to be in a relationship, much less start a family. This was supposed to be easier for both of them.

"What's with these guys who absolutely have to work when their girlfriend needs to see a doctor?" he mused out loud.

"Coincidence?" Luce offered. "Tillis would have to be a damn good actor. Somehow, I don't see him as a killer."

"I'm not sure we can rule him out yet, but I'd like to speak with Cory's boyfriend as well."

"Yeah, tomorrow." The shop where Cory had admired a dress was closed now, so that was going on the tomorrow list too.

Tyler held the door open for her, and they went inside.

"Murderers!" someone screamed.

❧

Luce had a plan. It was yet to be determined if it was a good one. She was aware that she had attracted some scrutiny—but she also knew they had to move fast.

"Good evening," she said to the receptionist. "Detectives Allen and Murphy. I'd like to speak to Dr. Jones if she's available?"

"Just a moment. I'll check," the woman promised and picked up her phone.

Luce turned to Murphy. "We can't overlook anything," she said. "I'll see what I can do, meanwhile you could ask around some more? Anything pertaining to patients being threatened? I think they were going after patients they knew were vulnerable."

"Both of them had somewhat of a support system. Cory did have someone to go with her," Tyler reminded her. "I'm not sure yet what you're getting at, but I'll give it a try."

At least he didn't seem to have a problem with her telling him what to do.

"Hi," Kendra said, sounding worried. "I hear you have bad news?"

"Can you talk for a bit?"

Kendra shrugged. "I'm on a break. A few minutes."

"Good."

"Detective Murphy," Tyler said. "We haven't met."

"Dr. Jones, but you know that already. Luce?"

"Yeah." She cast a quick look at Tyler who nodded and went on his way to question the woman at the reception desk. Luce followed Kendra into her office, aware of her questioning gaze when she closed the door. "You want to know if it's awkward working this particular case together...yes. Now that we got that out of the way, let's talk about Cory Baldwin. A witness saw her being pulled into a car. The girl can't give a good description, but we're sure Cory didn't go willingly. What can you tell me about her?"

"Luce." Her tone was suspiciously soft. "I know this is all extremely taxing, but there's not much I can tell you. If you need a patient's files, you have to go through the proper channels."

"And we will, but you know that time is of the essence, right? Cory's friend, Angelica, said that she scheduled an appointment, but she didn't know about the waiting period. There's a boyfriend we haven't spoken to yet. Same age, so it's unlikely that he has anything to do with the kidnapping, and besides, the friend would have recognized him. We're more interested in the protesters outside. Anything Cory might have shared with you?"

"I can tell you she didn't share much. Coffee?"

"Oh God, yes, please."

Kendra cast her a quick smile before she filled a cup for Luce. "I brought the one you gave me the other day. It's good. Anyway, Cory was adamant about the sex being consensual. And I shouldn't be telling you more than that, but if you want my opinion, the kidnapping is unrelated."

"How much of a vetting process do you have for employees? Someone who has access to those files and appointments, knows the medical history?"

"You're kidding me, right? You remember you go past a metal detector every time you come in?"

"I wasn't insinuating...Come on, you know that they try to infiltrate workplaces like yours."

"I know that, but I'll vouch for my colleagues. Luce, you're tired. You have a lot on your plate. Even I can see that Wendy Tillis and Cory have nothing in common."

"Except they were both pregnant. Both of them came here for an appointment, and they were both screamed at outside."

"Wendy came for prenatal care. Cory was here to schedule an abortion—" She shook her head in a frustrated gesture. "Don't try to fish for information please. If you get me that warrant, I'll hand over everything it says I have to hand over, but meanwhile, the privacy of the patients is priority."

"Even if you could save their lives?"

"That's low."

Luce had to admit it. "I'm sorry. I have the feeling that whoever was behind Wendy's disappearance, and took Cory, is escalating. Wendy's death might have been an accident, but sooner or later, they will likely kill someone. So, if you could make an exception, just this one time..."

"I can't. I'm sorry too."

"All right, then I guess that's it. If a patient mentions anything that's out of the ordinary, someone following them, threats, let me know."

"I will," Kendra said tersely. "I hope you can find her soon."

"You and me both."

She had to do better.

Chapter Twelve

Kendra wasn't wrong. Luce was tired and had been for a while. She wasn't sure when it had started, only that she couldn't afford to dwell on it now. Tyler had spoken to several employees who had given him the same, somewhat vague answers.

Yes, patients often felt uncomfortable or threatened. Usually, it didn't result in kidnapping and murder.

"There is no connection between Cory and Hyde or Peters." Tyler's frustration mirrored her own. "We have got to look somewhere else."

"The field. Did he drive Wendy there, and if that's the case, we could look into their vehicles if we had enough on either one of them. Or do they have property in the area?"

"There are farms. We looked."

"Yeah, I know. Let's swing by anyway."

Dusk was falling when, about fifteen minutes later, they stood in the same spot where Wendy Tillis's body had been found. Luce remembered the drug in her system. Someone wanted to make sure she didn't run...but from where?

They were surrounded by woods and farmland. The few scattered farmhouses were far away, one of them abandoned, the other families with no ties to the victims whatsoever. None of them had ever been to the Women's Health Center, as a patient or a protester. None of them raised any red flags.

Yet, she ended up here. It couldn't have been just a matter of convenience. Was it murder after all and he dumped her here? Did he think they wouldn't find her? That would have been an odd calculation. There were more people hiking in the area at this time of year.

Where did he come from?

"Tomorrow will be a long day. How about we grab a bit to eat and call it a night?"

"If you could just drop me off at my car?"

"Why are you avoiding me?" Tyler asked out of the blue.

This wasn't good, the two of them being alone in the middle of nowhere, and she still needed to catch a ride with him. The truth was, they didn't know each other that well. Even though she felt certain he would have reacted in a reasonable way, she didn't want to have that conversation. Ever.

"What are you talking about? Since you've been on this case, I've been spending most of my waking hours with you."

It wasn't a lie. Meanwhile she had made Kendra angry at her, when she was longing to have another girl's night in so badly. They, too, had a lot to talk about.

"It's true that we've been spending a lot of time together," he admitted as they were walking back to the car.

Luce looked back over her shoulder, hoping for some immediate inspiration that didn't come.

"I was thinking..."

"How's Susan?" she cut in.

"She's fine. And I think you misunderstood me that other time."

"What's there to misunderstand? I'm happy for you."

"When this case is over, do you think there will ever be a moment when we can talk? I know that we've been coasting on lots of coincidences, but what would be wrong with taking advantage of them?"

Everything. She forced a smile.

"This is a bit of a surprise. But you're right, we have to solve this first, and we still have ways to go."

"You don't think I'd hook up with just anyone?"

"At the conference? Isn't that what people do?"

"The conference. Then in the city where you happen to visit your cousin, and I happen to work. Now, here we are again...Some people would say it's fate or something."

"Well, I'm not some people. Can we go home?"

"Of course."

❦

In the precinct's parking lot, Luce waited in the driver's seat until Tyler was back in his own car. She waved as he passed her by and then left the car to head upstairs. She wasn't mad. She knew she wasn't that biased.

There was a pattern, somewhere between Peters and Hyde, Cory and Wendy.

She settled behind her computer once more, feeling a sense of relief at the quietude at this hour. Detectives were out on a case, or home.

Only Lieutenant Chomsky was still in her office, talking on the phone.

"Detective, I'd like to speak to you for a moment. Come with me?"

Luce jumped. She had focused so hard on the words and numbers on the screen she hadn't noticed Chomsky end the call.

"Of course. I haven't had the chance to apologize to D.A. Troy yet," she felt the need to say.

Chomsky made a dismissive gesture. "That's all right. Please sit."

Unsure what she was going to hear, Luce did.

"We're going to see the boyfriend tomorrow and ask for the security footage at the same time. We didn't get much from the clinic, but it's pretty much what we thought. Cory wanted to do this quietly before anyone found out. Of course, the folks waiting outside are never quiet."

"No, they aren't. That can take a toll."

"It's been taking a toll on patients and doctors forever, but there's nothing we can do about it. As D.A. Troy reminded me, the law allows it."

"I'll be honest with you."

That made Luce cringe. Nothing good could come after that, could it?

"You've been on a confrontational course since before this case. I think I've come to know you pretty well. You've been in this unit almost as long as it has existed, and you've been one of the most level-headed cops I've worked with. Can I ask you what happened?"

"Nothing happened. And besides, would you ask Ritter that question?"

Chomsky gave her a wry smile. "It's not Ritter I'm worried about. You know you were out of line with Troy. Looking at all the facts, I agree with you that they lead back to the clinic and the protesters, but you have nothing solid yet. I need you to be more careful, especially as you're getting closer to identifying a suspect."

"That's why I'm here," Luce said, hoping it didn't sound defiant and stubborn.

"I know. And I know you're good at what you do. Don't get distracted—and do try to get a good night's sleep every once in a while."

"That's hard to do when those women are out there." Plural? Did she really think that? "It's one thing to deal with a handful of trolls online. You can literally block them out. But this? They don't even ask why patients go inside, not that it's any of their business."

"I agree, it isn't. Like I said, I want you to be careful. For your sake, for the sake of this case, and to be honest, for mine. Something like the other day with Troy can't happen again. I don't want to lose you."

"You won't. I promise."

"All right. Go home, Allen. Tomorrow, bring me some results."

"Yes, Ma'am."

In her kitchen, Luce sat over the file she'd brought home, with a mug of coffee and a container of reheated leftovers. It was a small blessing that her stove and microwave still worked.

Peters' face stared back at her from the photo, and she remembered his parting words. Revealing intent—or did he talk to all women that way?

She wrote down the contact information of the woman who had pressed charges and then changed her mind, his ex-girlfriend. Tyler was right to some extent, this was a story completely different from Cory Baldwin's. Her father was unknown, her mother had been arrested on robbery charges and was serving a prison sentence.

She thought about Maggie Rowland, who paid babysitters so she could be a part of a loud irrational group that did nothing to help any children. Saw nothing wrong with having her daughter around a man silently—or sometimes with words—threatening other women.

Jared Hyde, who was certainly smarter than to believe the talking points he peddled—he just knew where to land them. He had a chance at becoming a state senator.

Why did everyone deny that this was a reason to be angry, to feel trapped in a system where politeness and comfort mattered more than people's lives?

She almost picked up the phone to call Kendra, before she remembered that Kendra might not want to talk to her tonight.

Something was turning her stomach, most likely an overdose of caffeine. Damn, this was already her only vice.

Luce abruptly closed the file, her vision blurring. She gave in to the inevitable. A few minutes. Tonight.

Tomorrow, she had to keep it together.

Chapter Thirteen

A t least they started the day with a small victory: The owner of the boutique where Cory had been window-shopping, handed over the security footage right away. Luce drove to the station to deliver it to the tech lab while Tyler went to interview Cory's boyfriend.

Luce didn't care to rehash their awkward conversation or last night's private meltdown. She dove right back into her research.

There had to be something to bring Peters back. His history indicated clearly that he was the most violent of the bunch. Luce didn't believe for a minute that him buying ice cream for children at the protest made him one of the good guys. He was still gleefully intimidating patients, or anyone who dared to set any boundaries for him.

She picked up the phone and called Sally Harper, the woman who had filed charges against him and then changed her mind.

Harper sounded mildly interested until Luce revealed the reason for her call.

"Didn't you do your homework, Detective? It was just a misunderstanding. I have nothing more to add."

"Ms. Harper, Mr. Peters is a person of interest in an ongoing investigation." That might be stretching it a little, but she didn't have a lot of options left. "I know the charges were dropped, but you could help us establish a pattern of behavior."

"What kind of pattern, that he's a jerk who runs with the holier-than-thou crowd?"

"You know about the protests?"

The woman laughed bitterly. "Honey, that's where we met. It was at a time when I still believed in that kind of thing."

"In your statement, you said he hit you and threatened you on several occasions. I'm sorry to ask, but did he ever confine you, keep you from leaving?"

Harper was silent for a few heartbeats. "That's oddly specific. I assume you have a reason for asking me that? What did he do?"

"Are you saying..."

"He was extremely jealous. That's why I wanted to leave, because it got too much. To your question, no, he didn't lock me in anywhere, but it wasn't hard to see that it was where we were headed. You know, the kind of guy who gives you all his attention, and a few months later he calls all women whores, and you know you made a colossal mistake?"

Luce was fortunate enough not to have experienced any of it, but then again, she didn't date all that often. She'd certainly say yes if Kendra ever asked her out on a date, but it wasn't likely, was it? And the question had no place here at work.

"None of this is your fault."

"Thank you for saying that. It didn't make much of a difference, did it?"

That was an uncomfortable avenue to venture down.

"Has he contacted you at all since the charges were dropped?"

"No, and I'm not interested in catching up. Are you going to tell me what you are suspecting him of?"

No need to scare her as long as Peters kept his distance.

"Like I said, he's a person of interest. Thank you, Ms. Harper. If there's anything else, please call me."

Tyler still hadn't returned from his interview, so, after taking a few notes, Luce went back to her search on Hyde. He was running an aggressive campaign, with all of his talking points rooted in fear. Some people's fear that "the other" could take over, that if others gained more rights, they would lose theirs.

Or perhaps some of them just liked the crass language Hyde used. His ads and videos were a lot less polite than the way he had acted at the station, she noticed. Unfortunately, once in power, he would be able to blend in while trying to enact every one of his horrific policy proposals.

Luce straightened in her chair. Yes, everyone around her was right. As bad as this was in the general sense, it was unlikely to help her bring back Cory. And Ashley. She massaged her forehead wearily, deciding she needed more coffee.

In the break room, she resisted the lure of the chocolate bar from the vending machine and went back to her desk. Harper's statement spoke to a violent pattern, but Troy wouldn't think it was specific enough. Luce leaned back in her chair as she sipped the coffee.

Buying ice cream for children. Cory was a teenager who had made an appointment to have an abortion.

Too vague.

Wendy Tillis didn't fit in.

She pulled up a map and marked the Tillises' address, and that of the group home. Then the clinic.

It was beyond frustrating. Nothing stood out.

Back to Hyde. Luce found an article that showed a picture of him going door to door campaigning. In some neighborhoods, it hadn't gone too well. People who understood what he was up to had slammed doors in his face, in some cases put up their own signs out front.

"I don't care much for the other guy either," a resident was quoted. *"But Hyde...He's the worst."*

Luce went back to her map. Okay. No reason to get excited yet—but she was. Her next call was to Steve Tillis. She kept her question vague.

"I suppose you have no news on who murdered Wendy?"

She hated to admit it. They might be getting closer though. She remembered Chomsky's warnings from the other night.

"I'm sorry. I was wondering if Wendy ever mentioned any political candidates coming to your door?"

"I'm not sure." He sounded confused. "What do you mean? She doesn't open the door to folks who want to sell anything, goods, politics, or religion. We have our own."

"But technically it would be possible? If she was home alone?"

"I think she would have...Wait, that Hyde guy. I think he was in the neighborhood once, but Wendy didn't mention anything, so I don't think he knocked on our door."

She cast another glance at the map after they'd ended the call. The group home wasn't in that particular circle, but it was only one of the places Hyde's campaign had gone.

On a whim, she pulled the names of a few streets and typed them into the search.

She found a couple of cases, a Rachel Benson, thirty-three, and Dawn Moreno, twenty-five, both reported missing within the last three months.

That should convince Troy that they should at least invite him over once more?

First though, she'd have to grovel. And not just with Liz Troy.

❦

She had to wait for almost fifteen minutes before getting Kendra on the phone.

"I can't talk for long," she said and paused. "Is everything okay?"

"Yes. Thanks. I mean...I wanted to apologize. It wasn't fair using our friendship that way."

"It wasn't," Kendra agreed with a sigh. "I understand you want to help those women. I do too."

"I know that. I promise you, when I'm back I'll have that warrant for you."

"I don't understand what you want with this anyway. Patients come for a multitude of reasons."

"I'll know it when I see it, and yes, I hear how that sounds. Kendra, I need a favor. I don't want any details, I'm going to provide the paperwork for that, but I need to know if a Rachel Benson and a Dawn Moreno were ever patients at the clinic."

"What?"

For a second, she thought that Kendra was going to yell at her, but she sounded tired when she spoke.

"I've been worried about Rachel," she said. "She had scheduled her appointment but never came back after the waiting period. I tried to call but didn't reach her. I figured she had changed her mind. It does happen."

Or someone decided to change it for her.

"You said you were worried?"

"She was really upset about the people outside, and having to wait, missing work for another appointment. I'm not sure about the other name, but I'll check it for you. I'll send you a text."

"Thank you so much, Kendra. I really appreciate it."

"I hope it helps. I have to go."

"Yes, for course."

Kendra had ended the call before Luce could say anything else. So, they were almost all right. She had to work on the rest after getting the pieces into place.

She had both Moreno's and Benson's case files in front of her when Tyler returned.

"You spent quite some time there. How did it go?" she asked, eliciting a shrug from him.

"As you can imagine. Guy has a job after school, and he went because he was worried his parents might find out he got a girl pregnant."

"Nice." The case made certain subjects come up between them with an alarming frequency. Her life would be so much more relaxed once they could solve it.

"Yeah. Anything out of the ordinary?"

"No, he doesn't know anything. I just had to stay a bit to keep the emerging family drama contained. His parents were not amused, and I don't blame them. With all the options available these days? You'd think they could be more responsible, but I guess that's teenagers for you."

Luce wondered if she had become prone to detecting jibes from the people around her, or if it was just Tyler she was specifically paying attention to. Either way, she didn't have a lot of patience for any of it these days. They might be working together again, stay friendly, have the occasional dinner.

They were not that good a match otherwise.

"You disagree?" he asked, likely picking up on her irritation.

"Maybe. It doesn't matter. I found a case of another woman going missing during the waiting period for a scheduled abortion. I'm waiting on confirmation of another one. They, and Wendy Tillis, all lived in the same neighborhood where Jared Hyde had been going door to door in the past few months."

"Wow."

"Is that a good or a bad wow?"

"It's a...I'm not sure. I thought you were pretty much sold on Peters. Hyde is an extremist for sure, but I don't see him as a killer. He's too careful for that, knows exactly how far he can go without getting his hands dirty."

"Wendy might have been an accident, remember? And maybe he has someone to do the dirty work for him. Like Peters."

"And they do what? What's the M.O. here, Luce?"

Her cell phone alerted her to the arrival of a text message.

Martin saw DM. Says she was afraid, had received threats before appointment. Didn't come back after waiting period.

Kendra hadn't added anything personal to the message, but her words made all the difference.

"Whoever is behind this, and I'm not ruling Peters nor Hyde out, they made a mistake with Wendy for some reason. The other ones, like Cory, all went missing during the waiting period. That's a small window. How do they know about it?"

"Wendy was the outlier, according to that theory. Why is she dead? She managed to get away? Or whoever did this didn't believe she was still pregnant?"

She could tell that Tyler still wasn't convinced. Or perhaps he was horrified at the idea that they'd find more bodies.

"Someone's targeting this clinic for some reason...maybe," he offered. "I don't think it gets more specific than that."

"I want to take it to Chomsky and Troy anyway. Something like this takes a planner. Peters is more the doer, but I wouldn't put it past Hyde to mastermind an idea like that."

"To kidnap several women he saw go into the clinic?"

It wasn't like she was comfortable with that notion, on the contrary. It was a rather horrific thought. But Luce had a feeling this might be exactly what they were looking at.

"Let's talk to Chomsky, see what she says."

Twenty minutes later, Luce cast Tyler a triumphant look as she picked up her phone to call Hyde's office.

"Hi, Ms. Grimm. It's Detective Allen again. I'm afraid I have to speak to Mr. Hyde right now."

She could basically hear the woman scowl, but she got her boss on the phone.

"Detective Allen. You must not have a lot of work to do if you have time to chat with me again. While I have you here, can I count on your vote?"

"I wasn't calling about your candidacy. A few more questions have come up, and I'd like you to come to the station one more time. Tomorrow morning?"

"Questions, you say. You can't do this on the phone?"

"I'd rather not. It's nothing for you to worry about, just something I'd like to confirm."

"I have to admit I'm curious."

She almost smiled. As much as Luce loathed everything he stood for, this was going in the right direction. She knew that appealing to his ego would do the trick.

"I'll see you tomorrow then. Thank you, Mr. Hyde. Have a good day."

"You too, Detective."

"See? We're staying polite. Troy will have nothing to complain about."

"We don't have a whole lot of time," Tyler reminded her. "The lieutenant would be happier if you dropped that line of investigation."

"But she understands we have to tie up some loose ends first. I swear it's going to be worth it. One way or another, he has something to hide."

Something they'd hopefully expose soon, because it wasn't looking good for other leads.

The security footage was grainy, showing Cory admiring that dress, then turning around as a car pulled up next to her, a non-descriptive dark van. There was a short exchange, the door opening and an arm shooting out to pull her in. She tried to resist, to no avail. The man hit the gas.

"I don't blame Angelica for not being able to give a good description." Luce groaned. "No license plate visible, and we have the most common type of vehicle and outfit on that man."

"Did it occur to you that he planned it exactly that way?" Tyler asked, and she glared at him.

"You're not suggesting I should have a sense of humor about any of it?"

"No. There's nothing funny about it. There's no point in getting frustrated either. We have no point of comparison. This is the moment Cory was taken. We know Wendy went to her car, left the clinic parking lot and showed up on one of the traffic camera, then we lose her trace. What about the others?"

"Three out of four went missing during the waiting period. This is relevant."

"I didn't even know such a thing existed here," Tyler admitted. "Why do politicians assume women can't make up their own minds?"

"That's too long of a discussion for the moment." Not that she ever wanted to get back to it.

Chapter Fourteen

D riving home later that day, Luce was happy to have avoided more awkward conversations, with her boss, her temporary partner, or the D.A. All of it counted as a win, though
restlessness had a tight grip on her, with a bit of guilt mixed
in. They were making progress, but not good enough, not fast
enough.

She was still convinced that her angle was a worthwhile one,
though she had to admit that the logistics of it would be tricky
for the perpetrator. Choosing the victims. Luce shuddered at
the thought that he was planning these abductions, setting up
a place to hold more than one at a time...to do what?

Luce let herself into the house, something indefinable making her hair stand on end the moment she walked over the
threshold. If she had been superstitious, she might have believed
in it being a sign.

Get a grip.

Perhaps the contractor had finally come by to start tackling
the remaining work? At least look at it?

She frowned at the dark spot on the side of the plastic tarp
still separating the kitchen and what would be her dining area
someday in the future. Walking closer, Luce noticed that there
was a stain on the floor as well. She pushed the plastic aside and
stepped into the other room, the sound of a person's breathing

the only warning she got. The man tackled her to the ground, but before she could turn and get a look at him, he jumped to his feet and ran.

What had she interrupted?

Luce scrambled to her feet as well, wincing at the pain shooting up her back. Her cell phone already in hand, she almost dropped it to the floor when she realized what was written on the drywall.

Murderer.

Her hands shook as she made the call.

Much to his credit, Ritter was there with a couple of uniforms ten minutes later. Good. She knew how to deal with him. There was no chance she would cry in front of him, and perhaps she could skip that step altogether.

"I'll take care of everything," he promised. "You want to check and see if something's missing? Is there anyone you can stay with tonight?"

"I'll take a look. I'll call someone later." She could have called her mother, stayed with her, but she'd have a lot of explaining to do. Luce wasn't ready. She chose the number that was always on top of her list as she started to examine the rooms.

"Hi, Kendra, it's me again. I was wondering if I could crash at your place tonight. I promise you won't even realize I'm there."

"Luce, of course. What happened?"

Apparently, she didn't sound as cool and detached as she'd hoped.

"There was a break-in at my house. My colleagues are here right now. I'll explain later."

"A break-in? Are you okay? You didn't surprise them?"

"I'm fine. I promise. Talk to you later."

Ending the call, Luce cast a glance at the literal writing on the wall.

"Looks like blood," Ritter stated the obvious. "Do you have any idea where this could have come from?"

"No. No idea."

"You ever had to pull the trigger on someone? I'm not saying anyone had the right to do this, but we have to look at the possibilities..."

"I know you have to ask this, but no. I haven't shot anybody."

"All right. You know this will take a while. You have an extra set of keys? I could give them back to you tomorrow."

"Yes. Give me a minute. I'll pack something...so far, I don't think anything's missing, but it doesn't look like that's what he was here for."

"I'm really sorry, Allen. Hope you can get this fixed soon."

"Yeah. Thanks for everything."

She walked back up to her bedroom where she threw a few clothes into a carry-on suitcase. On her way out, Luce picked up the extra key and handed it to Ritter.

"Where are you on Ashley Johnson?" she asked.

"Not much progress, I'm afraid. That girl has fallen off the face of the Earth."

What other answer had she expected on a day like this?

It wasn't the first time Luce wished she could snap her fingers and men like Danes, or Hyde, simply wouldn't exist. Or the man who had waited for her when she came home, his intent unclear. Was it, really, or would she sleep better tonight believing it?

❧

"Luce, I'm so sorry." Kendra greeted her at the door with a brief hug, too brief. Luce wished she could lean into her warmth a little longer, but Kendra was in doctor mode as much as she was in friend mode.

"Tell me what happened? Are you all right?"

"I am." She gritted her teeth against the residual pain from having been knocked to the floor. It could have been worse. "He just pushed me and ran."

"He was still in the house?" Kendra's eyes widened. "Waiting for you?"

"Please, don't make me picture that any more than I already have. My colleagues suggested not to spend the night, so here I am."

"Of course. Sit. Can I get you anything to drink? Dinner's almost ready."

"I missed this," Luce said out loud before she could stop herself.

"Me, cooking for you? You could have just said so."

The smile vanished from her face when she looked at Luce, making her wonder what Kendra was seeing.

She reached out, her fingers curling around Luce's wrist. "That's blood. Is there something you're not telling me?"

"Probably, but I was hoping I could take a hot shower first. It's not my blood. We don't know yet. Someone smeared slurs across the wall. You know how it goes. They'll take it to the lab...There's nothing much I can do tonight." Considering that reality, she was using a lot of words.

"Go ahead. We can talk some more later."

Luce was already on the bottom stair before Kendra had finished her sentence. Whoever's blood it was, getting out of that shirt had become an urgency. In the guest bathroom, she stripped and stepped into the stall, breathing a sigh of relief when the hot water cascaded down her body. The water pressure was much better than at her house, another thing she'd have to take care of eventually. She leaned back against the tiled wall, willing herself to do this quick so she wouldn't have to time to obsess about the possibilities.

If this was related to the missing women, and it was likely, the man who had defaced her wall meant to send a warning. Or he'd been sent by someone else, someone with money and connections.

How far they would go for that warning was yet unclear.

She hurried to get into a new set of clothes and went back down. The smell of food that promised to be delicious almost made her knees buckle, reminding her she'd had mostly coffee since breakfast.

"Thank you for letting me crash here...and all of his," Luce indicated the table. "You have a lot on your plate too."

"At least it's been some time since one of them followed me home."

They were both silent for a few seconds, the gravity of her words more than sobering.

"I'll be talking to Hyde tomorrow. Maybe after that, Troy will be more open to getting me warrants."

"She's around a lot for someone in her position," Kendra remarked. "I'm no expert, but wouldn't an A.D.A. usually handle these communications?"

Luce had had similar thoughts, but she had an idea. "Danes has become a high-profile case. She wants that conviction. I do too, obviously. But she also has ambitions, and going hard on the protesters will not earn her any political points in her circle. Anyway...let's just forget about them for a couple of hours."

"That's a good idea." Kendra reached out to squeeze her shoulder gently, the contact pure bliss. Her wistful smile, however, told Luce what she already knew—with the two of them having sworn their respective oaths, and believing in them, it wouldn't be easy to forget.

It was good to know that Ritter was still looking. She would do the same.

Luce needed to clear her head from the evening's volatile surprise. Kendra's presence always helped, no matter how stressful her day had been.

"Unfortunately, I can't cook like that, but I swear one day we'll have time, and I'll take you to your favorite restaurant. All the courses included."

"Luce Allen is going to take me on a date?" Kendra sounded intrigued which was both reassuring and alarming to Luce, and neither one made much sense. They were adults. She knew Kendra dated women exclusively. Kendra might remember she had once expressed interest in dating a woman.

"Would that be such a bad idea?"

"I don't know, you tell me."

It might be the fact that tonight could have gone in various bad ways, but it gave Luce both clarity and courage.

"It might be. Or it could be a great idea. One way or another, this case will be over at some point, and I won't come badgering you for more information. I'm really sorry about that by the way. I shouldn't have done that."

"I already accepted your apology." The hint of amusement to her tone that was gone the next moment. "This has nothing to do with it. And you know, a warm meal and bed don't come with conditions, especially on a night where you were attacked in your own home. There's been a lot going on in your life and mine. We should take it easy."

"Can't I do something nice for you for a change? I was talking about dinner."

She could feel her cheeks warm. Luce realized she had no choice but to back-paddle on the subject, because the conversation could get uncomfortable any moment.

The day she told Kendra that she wasn't going to call Tyler to fill him in on her decision, Kendra had been nothing but supportive. She dealt with everything and everyone on a case-by-case basis, something Luce agreed with in theory. Unfortunately, they disagreed on Luce's current situation.

How could she make it clear that her feelings for Kendra had nothing to do with any of it? Or at least, not anymore. Now, these feelings existed in a wondrous world of their own, one she often wished she could explore without ruining their friendship.

A fling away from home that had ended in consequences and decisions to make belonged in another world, and she had dealt with it. Everything else—coincidence. Tyler might be interested in giving whatever had attracted them to each other, another try. She wasn't.

"Of course we can have dinner. But you're nearly falling asleep over this one. Dessert, and we call it a night?"

Kendra was giving her an easy way out. It might be what friends did after one of them was attacked in their home? While Luce appreciated the gesture, the pang of disappointment was just as real.

"Sounds good," she said.

She couldn't be petty when, after Luce had basically harassed her for information, Kendra went all in to make her comfortable?

Perhaps it was all her, and she simply couldn't do comfortable, no matter how much she needed it.

Luce couldn't deny that the coffee and warm chocolate cake with ice cream did go a long way to calm her overactive nerves.

"This is heaven. I'm also surprised that my favorite friend who is a doctor, approves it."

Back to a more familiar, less suggestive tone. Kendra knew she had become the favorite the day they met.

"Since I am your friend, I know that you don't smoke, barely drink, and you eat better than most of the people I've seen in your profession or mine. We're not going to make this a habit."

"The break-in? I don't need that again." A muscle in her back twitched painfully at the reminder. "This cake? I'll be back for it."

"You are incorrigible," Kendra stated.

Luce wasn't going to deny the charge.

For a moment, she had worried that her awkward, be-tween-the-lines offer would make Kendra send her to the gue-stroom. To her relief, Kendra had no such intentions.

And why would she? It wasn't like Luce would be making a move on her, on a day like this. She needed to sleep, clear her brain, start over.

Figure out a way to pin Hyde down, bring those missing women home.

Piece of cake.

This is why she had a problem with comfort, Luce thought as she was blinking tears away. It made her let her guard down. She couldn't have that, not yet.

Chapter Fifteen

A king size bed was perfect for someone who was and wanted to remain in denial. For a grown woman who had found herself in a number of tricky situations, Luce had been quite good at it, ignoring the obvious, evading the questions that had been on her mind since the beginning.

She had dated a couple of women, one in college, one shortly after, and then stopped...Why, she wasn't sure, and she had never questioned it. She had acknowledged the attraction and wasn't trying to hide it. Her reluctance might have to do with the fact that the world was more likely to give her peace if she stayed under the radar. Just a fact.

It had nothing to do with pride, or what she considered to be real and good.

At this moment, her evasions only contributed to the chaos in her mind, missed chances, in private and on the job...There might be a solution to it all. If that was the one, she didn't want to waste any more time to find out.

Despite her determination, Luce fell asleep over those musings. As usual, she felt warm and comfortable in this room, in the presence of someone she had come to appreciate more than anyone in her life.

She woke sometime during the night, warmer than usual, with Kendra's arm draped around her waist. Coincidence, most likely, even though it had never happened before. While she enjoyed the closeness, Luce wasn't sure if she should wake her, or if that would make things even more awkward.

Meanwhile, she might just as well try to relax, breathe in the scent of soap and shampoo, familiar and enticing...

Kendra moved, and a heartbeat later, her hand was in Luce's hair, the touch gentle and more sensual than a friend's would be. Luce leaned in to kiss her, her heart hammering, leaving her with no doubt as to how much, and how long she had wanted this. Kendra didn't pull away, on the contrary. Her lips opened easily, and then she kissed Luce back. It was everything she ever imagined, and more, the gentle intimacy making all the stress of the past few weeks fall away...

If only it was that easy. It was Luce who broke the kiss.

"I'm so sorry," she said. That might be a lie, but it seemed the right thing to say.

Kendra brushed a finger over her lips, making her shiver.

"I'm not," she said.

"I didn't mean to ambush you."

"I understand. But with all those messages we've been sending between the lines, it was hardly an ambush."

Could this really mean what she hoped it did?

"Now what?" she asked.

"Now we sleep, and tomorrow we make a plan for when you take me out to that restaurant," Kendra returned. "Then we talk...and whatever happens..."

"Could we skip straight to whatever happens?"

"No." Kendra tightened her arms around Luce. "I could have lost you today. I need a moment...if we really want to do this."

Luce didn't have to think twice about it. "I want to," she said.

She still didn't like letting her guard down but given that here with Kendra was the only space she could do it had to mean something. Or maybe it meant everything.

"I'm sorry, I need to be at the station early. Hyde's coming in."

"You'll be okay with that? After what happened?"

Leaning against the counter, Luce turned away from Kendra's scrutiny as she sipped her coffee.

"I'm fine. I'll just check in with Ritter to see if they found something already, but I doubt it."

"You're a cop. Wouldn't that break-in and assault, not to mention the creepy message, be priority?"

"They'll do the job," Luce assured her. Up until this moment, she would have doubted she was anyone's priority. But Kendra made it very clear that she cared. Ritter, while not chummy with any colleagues, was decent.

She'd get through this day.

"You think about which restaurant you prefer? I'll call you tonight."

"Sure. You really don't want to stay for breakfast? A few minutes won't make a big difference."

Kendra's offer was tempting—but if she sat down to eat, they might start having that conversation. Luce preferred to deal with Hyde first. The closer they got to solving this case, the sooner her and Tyler's teamwork would come to an end.

"Another day," she promised. "Thank you for the coffee...and everything."

Kendra gave her a soft smile in return.

Today, the world was a bit brighter.

Another coffee in hand, Luce stood in front of the two-way mirror, studying Jared Hyde who stared back at her as if he knew she was there. Given his previous run-in with the authorities, he probably guessed—or perhaps he had watched a few crime dramas.

"Are you ready?" Tyler asked.

"I am. Let's give him a few more minutes."

Narcissism, anger, the need for attention, all of it could make an explosive mix that could erupt at any time. When it did, Troy might believe her.

Luce could recognize how she, too, had been caught up in the emotionality of it all, the tension caused by strangers who saw it as their prerogative to overrule any plans she had for her own life—her plans, and those of others. Someone in their midst was willing to end a life as long as they got their will.

Life of a mother.

In the end, her feelings weren't that important, and neither were the egos of Hyde, Peters and any of them...Bringing those women home, finding justice for Wendy Tillis.

Nothing else mattered.

"Let's do this," she said, depositing her empty paper cup into the garbage bin.

Tyler followed her into the room where Luce didn't lose any time.

"Mr. Hyde, thank you for coming. We know you're a busy man, but you could really help us."

"You're joking, aren't you? Damn right I am busy working for the people of my state. If you really acknowledged that, you wouldn't keep dragging me in here."

"Oh, I don't think anyone dragged you here, but let's save some time. Zach Peters."

Tyler cast her a surprised look.

"What about him? Like me, he exercises his constitutional rights."

"Nothing wrong with that. Have you ever seen him engage in inappropriate ways? Attack anyone?"

"Attack, that's a strong word, Detective. You tell me, what's the right way to deal with a murderer?"

Luce kept her back straight and her gaze neutral though she was overly aware of the shiver skittering down her spine. Too many coincidences, even though he wasn't the only one who favored a certain terminology.

"See, that's where we differ, Mr. Hyde. I define it based on the law, not ideology. You're saying you never observed anything out of the ordinary with Mr. Peters?"

Hyde shrugged. "I'm not sure how you pegged me for the expert. I'm a guy running for state senate I'm not a shrink. But if my opinion is worth that much to you, he's one of the good guys. Quiet. A soldier."

Metaphorically—they knew that Peters hadn't served.

"He works on your campaign?"

"Not that I know of. A couple of Defenders came to volunteer for me, but I'm not aware of everyone, if that was a trick question."

"Oh, we don't do trick questions. We know he's been to your office a few times."

"So what? Overlapping interests."

"Sure. You remember going door to door on the 5th of the month, in Park View"

"Of course. It was quite successful. People are tired of being canceled for their values, and many pledged their support."

"What about Wendy Tillis?"

"What do you mean? I don't remember seeing her that day."

"Okay. What about her? Did she pledge to vote for you?" she asked, laying a photograph in front of him.

He studied Rachel Benson's picture with a smug grin. "Attractive lady. Did you talk to her? I think I offered her a new perspective on many things."

Based on what Luce knew about Rachel, she was certain that this was a bold-faced lie.

"And this woman?" She caught the hint of recognition on his face when she showed him Dawn Moreno's picture. "Did you offer her a new perspective as well?"

"Oh, I remember her. Slammed the door in my face." He laughed. "Can't get them all, can you?"

"What do you do about the ones you don't get?"

Tyler cleared his throat. "What my colleague means to say is, aside from going door to door—"

"What I meant to say is, if they don't see things your way, what measures do you take? Show up at their house again? Doxx them?"

"What do you think? I don't have time for this nonsense. I try to reason with people, but I'm not a shepherd looking for lost sheep. Some people are just that...lost. Sheep. They will come to their senses eventually."

"Three women have disappeared within a matter of weeks, inside a small perimeter where you've been campaigning. That's quite the coincidence, don't you think?"

"What would I want with them?"

"You tell me. Trying to, what you call 'reason' with them? Because you object to their right to have an abortion?"

Hyde gave her a hard stare. "You're right, I object. However, I am not as stupid as you think. What a waste of time it would be to try and convince them one by one—that's the mistake you liberal types always make. We organize. We know who's on our side, who we can count on. I want to change laws, not opinions."

He was sweating.

Luce had finally found a way to be in the same room with him and still breathe.

She smiled. "Please, tell me more about how you're going to do that."

Chapter Sixteen

"This has got to stop," Liz Troy declared at the briefing following Hyde's interview. "You keep treading a fine line, and you get nothing from it."

"Four women!" Luce hadn't bothered sitting down. Tyler had taken a seat next to Troy, across from Lieutenant Chomsky. "All of them connected to the same clinic. One of them is dead. Why do you think this is nothing?"

Deep breath, she told herself.

"He keeps walking out of here, doesn't he?"

"D.A. Troy, Detective, please." Chomsky's irritation rang clearly.

"He's playing us. He lied about not seeing Wendy Tillis that day. He lies every time he opens his mouth, except that part about changing laws."

"Can you prove it?" Chomsky asked calmly.

"This would be the right time for surveillance."

Luce saw Troy shake her head.

"It's not enough, Allen!"

No one paid attention to the knock on the door. Ritter walked inside. "Hey, Allen. I got some news on the break-in at your house."

"What break-in?" Tyler and Chomsky asked almost in unison. Despite the seriousness of the situation, Luce barely suppressed a laugh. The irony of it all.

"I was going to tell you later. Excuse me for a moment? Let's go to my desk," she told Ritter who seemed unaware of his words' impact.

It was unlikely that she could have kept the incident a secret, but she would have preferred to choose the time to address the subject.

"Okay, what is it?"

"Some good news," Ritter told her. "That definitely wasn't human blood. Pig's to be precise."

"All right. Anything else?"

"They came through the window. You should really get that fixed."

"Thanks for the tip. Can I call someone to go there?"

"Sure. Whenever you're ready."

"Thanks. I have to go back in now."

"Good luck," he said. "Call me when you have a moment. There's been a development with Johnson as well."

Forget about the doubts. Everything was brighter this morning. She'd take a moment during her lunch break to call Kendra. She might have found the lighter side by accident, but Luce was determined to stay on it a bit longer.

She agreed with Ritter too—It was good news that the intruder hadn't smeared her wall with human blood. She couldn't wait to hear where he was on Ashley's case.

❧

Much as she had wanted to, Luce didn't manage to make that call or even send a text message. She had a quick lunch with Tyler where they discussed Hyde's interview.

"I'm torn," he said. "You make a few good points, but unfortunately Troy is right. We still don't have enough, and we're running out of time."

"So, we just give up? He's involved somehow. I know I overstepped with Troy the other day, but that has nothing to do with it. Hyde and Peters have something to do with the disappearances."

"Just because you say so, doesn't make it so. Nor does evidence magically appear."

"You're frustrating," she said the first thing that came to mind.

"Not so long ago, you didn't mind."

"That's when I didn't have to work with you." Luce stopped herself, hoping he wouldn't see that as an invitation to explore more private areas of their lives together. "What I mean is—"

"I hear you," he said, all joking gone from his tone. "About that break-in. Why didn't you tell me?"

"You know we had to get started with Hyde. No opportunity before Ritter blurted it out."

"What about last night?"

"I stayed at a friend's house. Really, I'm okay."

To her relief, Tyler didn't express any doubts or desire to pursue that particular subject further.

"What does your gut say?" he asked. "Do you think either one of them is involved in the break-in?"

"He wore a mask, like the man who took Cory. It was very fast, but judging from the body type, it could be either one. Or someone they paid. I'm more inclined to think that Hyde would be someone to pay for a job like that." And he emphasized the word "murderer." "All those disappearances within a short time, there is no way those aren't linked somehow."

"I'll give you that. However—"

Her cell phone rang, interrupting Tyler.

Dr. Martin was on the other end.

"Detective, I'm sorry I couldn't get back to you until now, but I had to check some things. You inquired about Dawn Moreno?"

"That's right. What can you tell me?"

"She was extremely upset when we first met. I suppose I can tell you, because it's not about her medical history. She said she was sure that someone was watching her and had followed her that morning. She got phone calls, text messages...I'm not sure if she involved the police. I advised her to do so."

Dawn Moreno had never filed that complaint, because she disappeared before she had the opportunity.

"Thank you, Dr. Martin. By any chance, did she mention a Jared Hyde? Or Zach Peters?"

Dawn had lived alone, like Rachel Benson. No electronics found which made the search more complicated.

"That politician, yes. She mentioned him coming to her door, him and another guy. They got quite rude."

The images evoked made Luce's stomach turn. If Dawn had reported him...Then what? He would have unleashed his sleazy lawyers, and Troy would have dropped the case?

She still wished Dawn had filed a report.

"Thank you. This is very helpful."

Luce had barely ended the call when her phone rang again. This time, it was Ritter.

"Where are you?" he asked. "We have a location for Danes. I thought you wouldn't want to miss that."

"You thought right. Thanks. You haven't left yet?"

"Just getting ready."

"All right. I'll be there in ten. Sorry," she said to Tyler. "I've got to go. I'll pay you back later?"

Luce didn't wait for an answer. This wasn't just a fluke, it was becoming a trend: Things were starting to look up.

She met with Ritter in the parking lot.

"You can ride with me," he said. "I'll fill you in on the way."

Luce had no objections, elated that this story was finally coming to an end. Danes had fooled them for long enough, trying to lure young girls to his place while pretending he was one of them.

They should have caught him much earlier.

Ritter detailing his most recent findings was sobering. He had finally traced Danes to the property of a distant cousin, who might or might not be aware of Danes' secrets. Luce shuddered at the thought of how long it had been for Ashley Johnson.

"Any sign of life?" she asked.

"We'll have to see." Ritter's curt answer was familiarly unemotional, but she could tell he was tense. Getting Danes off the streets was a big deal, for both of them, for the department.

Most of all, for Ashley Johnson.

Danes' cousin owned a couple of factories. The location was a warehouse currently not used by the company. Witnesses had seen several men, including Danes, go in and out.

It made Luce want to groan. "Why didn't they come forward earlier?"

Ritter shrugged. "It didn't seem strange to them at first. Then one of the neighbors recognized Danes...People have all kinds of reasoning, and we can't arrest them for that."

"Sometimes I wish we could, especially if a teenage girl's life is at stake."

"Me too," he made a rare admission. "And here we are."

Luce's stomach did flip-flops as she recalled the last time they got close to Danes. She knew that they had crossed all t's and dotted all i's that time, because she'd been in charge of it.

Ritter didn't care any less, but Danes had evaded them.

The door of the building was secured with a padlock.

They waited for the tactical team to breach the entrance and move in before they followed them inside.

For a few seconds Luce stood, disappointment almost a physical blow.

How was that possible? Again? The expanse of the concrete floor was empty. She heard heavy footsteps from the floor above, one of their colleagues shouting, "Clear!"

Ritter muttered a curse under his breath as they walked further inside, examining every corner.

Luce turned around, another time, until she felt the first signs of dizziness.

Then it came to her.

"Don't you think it looks bigger from the outside?" she asked.

"What, you think there's a hidden door somewhere?"

"I don't know, but it would be one reason the neighbors were slow on the uptake? Where exactly did they see Danes?"

"The front entrance, I suppose? Wait."

He jogged ahead of her to the other end of the warehouse where sunlight came in through a window high up. Luce followed close behind. There was no other door or window in the structure, but...She could smell it.

"Fresh paint," she said as she took a closer look at the back wall.

"There's something behind this. The warrant is good for the entire building, so let's see what it is."

She knocked on the wall, then again, a few inches to the right. "There's something hollow here." *Please, don't let it be a dead body*. She wasn't entirely sure who she was pleading to. Not the same God as the people who thought Wendy had brought death on herself because she walked into the Women's Health Center for prenatal care. Definitely not that God. "Let's get it open."

Upon further inspection, they discovered a mechanism that let part of the wall slide away to reveal a hallway and stairs.

"Classic."

She had to agree with Ritter. "Let's see what's down there."

Nothing on the outside could have prepared them for the space at the bottom of the stairs. They walked further into another hallway, and then a maze, multiple doors in either direction.

"Whatever this is, I doubt Danes's cousin doesn't know about it. Someone built it like this on purpose, probably before there was a factory, and not for something legit."

He stopped there, but Luce could guess what he was thinking. They had assumed that Danes was working on his own. This was starting to look like an entirely different story.

Behind them, more cops followed, their flashlights casting shadows as they went. Luce tried a door handle only to find it locked.

They all were.

She took another couple of steps before she froze at hearing the particular sound. A shot rang out, and she spun around, seeing Ritter on the ground. She reacted instinctively, returning fire as she rushed to his side. Rapid footsteps alerted them to someone fleeing the scene.

Ritter was conscious but looking ghostly pale in the light of her flashlight, clutching his thigh as she passed on the dreaded message through the microphone, *Officer down*. Blood was seeping through his fingers.

Luce shrugged out of her Kevlar vest and shirt, balled up the latter and pressed it against the wound. He took over as she put her vest back on over her tank top and directed the arriving backup.

"You better not die," she chided, though her heart was hammering. "This was expensive."

"Always a hoot, Allen."

"Yeah, that's me. Help is on the way."

They could hear voices on the other side of the door, crying.

"Go," he told her. "I'm not going anywhere."

"Yeah, right."

With Ritter bleeding profusely, and backup just moving in, Luce didn't have time to dwell on her own emotions. She all but jumped to her feet.

"We're the police," she yelled. "Who's there?"

"Please, help us." Not Ashley's voice, but the girl sounded about her age.

"Can you step away from the door?"

"Yes. I'll have everyone go in the other room."

"We'll get you out of there. It's going to be a little loud, okay?"

The lock didn't stand a chance, and the door sprang open, a hole where the handle had been.

Behind it, a group of girls and young women hesitantly stepped closer. They looked shell-shocked. Luce felt her knees go weak with relief when she recognized Ashley Johnson.

"My name is Luce Allen," she said. "We're here to bring you home."

Chapter Seventeen

The man who had shot at them wasn't Danes. He was one of six that had been arrested as their colleagues moved in. More arrests would follow in the afternoon.

Troy's office had no problems with any warrants regarding Danes's cousin and associates.

Before heading back to the station, Luce went to the hospital with Ritter. The waiting room was already starting to fill up with family and other cops.

"Go back to work," he said from the gurney. "Just don't take all the credit."

"Funny. You ruined my shirt." She shivered with just the tank top under her jacket. "All right. I'll check back in later."

"Ashley Johnson was among the girls," he said. "You were always right about Danes." She couldn't remember him addressing her with this hint of admiration in his tone. Ever.

"Yeah, I was. We'll discuss it later."

"I'd appreciate that," the doctor told her. "I need to take care of this gentleman now."

Luce left the hospital, remembering she had never called Kendra back. She hadn't updated Tyler either, but she supposed the latter could wait until she was back at the station.

She wondered if Kendra expected a call. If it was too late, she'd go with a text message.

Ashley Johnson would be going home, and so would the other girls. That was the bright spot of the day.

Luce couldn't ban the haunted gazes of those girls from her mind.

"This will take a while to clean up." Lieutenant Chomsky's words encompassed today's operation and the consequences that would go far beyond this day. "But thanks to the work you and Ritter have done, they have a chance at a future now."

"We still don't have Danes."

Troy shook her head. "You don't know how to take a win, do you? Those computers and files, the set-up of the building, it's a treasure trove. It will take days to get through all of it, and meanwhile, we have the girls' testimony. This is much bigger than Danes."

Luce had to agree. It also meant more victims, more trauma. At least she had no doubt that Troy wanted these men behind bars just as much.

"They have better attorneys too." She couldn't help it.

"So what? I know how to do my job. They won't send those attorneys for the foot soldiers."

The term soldier stuck with her, making her think of when Hyde used it for Peters, almost with an air of admiration. How did they not already have a paper trail leading to a possible connection?

Rowland had claimed Peters wasn't part of the Defenders who financed part of Hyde's campaign. But everything Hyde did and said was deliberate.

"Figure that part out," Chomsky advised. "Meanwhile, I'm grateful that Detective Ritter will make a full recovery. Since he's out for the time being, I asked Meyers and Crayden to help with the interrogations over the next few days. Allen…"

"You're not taking me off the Hyde case?"

"I wouldn't call it that just yet," Chomsky said dryly. "It was Ritter's idea to invite you back, and I'm sure he considers it a great one, given what you did today. You worked on Danes' case before he took Ashley. I think this makes only sense."

"What about the others? There's a pattern, and it concerns the protesters at the clinic."

"That's your theory," Troy said, unimpressed when Luce glared at her. "You had your eye on those four to begin with, and while their methods might leave much to be desired, they haven't done anything illegal."

"Peters threatened me!"

"Hold on, when did that happen?" Chomsky asked.

"The first time he came in. He *advised* me to let this go."

"But he has an alibi for last night?"

"I didn't check that with Ritter yet. We were a little busy dodging bullets."

"Okay." The lieutenant sighed. "This is what we'll do. Detective Murphy will continue on the disappearances. If he needs any additional help, I'll make sure he'll get it. I want you, Meyers, and Crayden to start on the interrogations, see if you can get anyone to talk."

"I'll bet you that most of them have a rap sheet already." Liz Troy seemed satisfied.

On the bright side, Luce would likely get out of having to apologize to her. Part of her wanted to believe them, that they could all take a moment to convince themselves and be grateful about the fact that the system still worked. To some extent.

She had to admit she was tired. She needed some sort of affirmation.

"I'll talk to Crayden and Meyers, check in with Murphy, and then we can get started," she said.

No one disagreed with her. For once.

❧

After today, Luce would have been okay to let Crayden take the lead. Since they were in the interrogation room with Danes's cousin Kenneth, and she had been on the case longest, it was up to her. Kenneth Danes's lawyer was with him, and they had agreed to talk.

"First of all, I want you to know that my client hasn't had any business in this area in years, and he's not close to his cousin either. So, this should be quick."

Luce shared a quick smile with her colleague before she turned back to the older cousin. "We'd appreciate quick. Just to clarify, does that mean you had no idea about the trafficking ring being run out of a warehouse you own?"

The attorney nodded, and Danes spoke.

"I own it on paper only. Haven't been there in months. It was about to be demolished."

"This property has been in your possession how long, ten, twelve years? Were you aware of the odd specifics, the connected underground space?"

"Not at all. I understand that you have to ask, Detective, but you have to see, my business is in constant flow. I buy and sell property as needed for storage. This one, we didn't need anymore, but we couldn't get the right buyer either. A few more weeks, and the demolition crew would have moved in. I was in there maybe once or twice, and I can assure you I wasn't looking for any hidden doors."

"Fair enough. Let's talk about your cousin then. You were interviewed last month when he disappeared?"

"Yes, and I'll tell you the same thing I told the other detective. Ryder, it was?" Luce didn't correct him, and he continued, "Joe and I haven't spoken in years. I want to be very clear. I don't know anything about his private life, and if he's involved in trafficking teenagers, I sure as hell didn't know about that either."

"Thank you for volunteering all that information," Luce said. "This will make my colleague's and my life a lot easier indeed."

His smile appeared genuine. It was the only genuine thing she'd seen from him today.

"I'm glad to help. Can I go now?"

"I'm afraid there's one little problem. Every single one of those girls identified you."

That was a bit of an exaggeration. Some had been too afraid. They still had enough.

"That's bull!" he raged, an abrupt change in demeanor that made Crayden, and the attorney, flinch. "They're lying."

Perhaps Luce was past the ability to react to the brazen entitlement of men like him. They hadn't even gone into much detail yet with the kidnapped girls. The threats he had made to them that she was aware of made her stomach turn, but she knew what made people like him tick.

"Why would they, Mr. Danes? What do you think they have to gain? You don't have to answer that."

"In fact, my client isn't going to answer any more of your questions," the attorney cut in.

"Not even if he could help himself? We're still looking for Joe. The D.A. is observing us, and she and I both hate loose ends."

He and the attorney shared a look. Danes was back to his calm, smug demeanor.

"That's not my problem, though, is it? I think we're done here."

"You're right," Crayden agreed. "But you have a multitude of other problems, and if you're willing to work with us on finding Joe…Well, let's say some of them might not be so bad."

That, too, was bending the truth. With the evidence they'd found in the underground part of the building, there was very little leeway for him.

His smile deepened. "Screw you," he said.

Luce could have sworn the attorney was fighting the urge to roll his eyes.

"As you wish," she said, getting up. "Too bad for you that most of the girls have already agreed to testify—and your accomplices are falling over themselves to save their hides. Smarter, if you ask me."

"Is that all, Detectives?"

"Yes, for now. Your client remains under arrest, of course."

Troy was right, this was a win. Luce assumed that over the next few days, more personnel would come in, perhaps even FBI, depending on what else was on those computers.

It would give her a chance to keep an eye on her and Tyler's case.

⁕

He was still at his desk when Luce returned to hers to pick up her coat and keys. Instead, she slumped into her chair, lifting her hand to her mouth to cover a yawn she couldn't suppress.

"Big day, huh?" Tyler commented.

"No kidding. Did you find anything new?"

"It's moving slow," he admitted. "I'm not averse to your theory, but we have very little to connect the victims. Not saying it's nothing."

"Yeah."

"That's all?"

"Grabbing a girl off the street, I don't see someone like Hyde do it. Peters, maybe, but if that's the case, they're pretty good at hiding the evidence. Hyde called him a soldier. A metaphor? Are there more?"

"Why would they target this specific clinic?"

"They have to start somewhere? The place was in the news quite a bit, first the bomb threat, then the arrest..."

"I don't know, it still seems...amateurish. This is why bomb guy was a single perpetrator. People like Hyde, and even Peters, are more organized, with different agendas. You heard Peters. He wants to change laws."

"If they hold those women, they have to keep them somewhere. Wendy escaped, but what if the others are still in that place? What if Wendy's death really was an accident?"

It had been a long day for Tyler too, but she could tell he was intrigued.

"That rules out punishment as the M.O. for murder," he reminded her.

"He might not have intended to kill her," Luce suggested.

"What else?"

"He wants to prevent them from having an abortion. That's the punishment and the M.O. in one."

Tyler stared at her with a mix of disbelief and admiration.

"I'm not sure if you're on to something, or if I'm about to go down a rabbit hole with you. Either way, I'm going to need food first."

"I can do that. Just let me make a quick call."

"Sure, go ahead."

Luce walked towards the exit while Tyler turned off his computer, out of earshot. Kendra picked up on the second ring.

"Hey."

"Luce, hi." Just hearing her voice made Luce breathe a little easier.

"Do you know what time you'll be home?" Kendra asked.

For a moment, confusion got the better of her, that, and an entirely more pleasant emotion. Luce couldn't indulge in either one as she remembered that she had invited herself to Kendra's home.

"It's been quite the day. I'm just now catching up with Tyler."

Why was there a hint of guilt creeping into her tone? This was about work. It was important. Kendra would be the first to understand.

"Sure," was the only response.

"I won't be late. And thanks again for harboring me. I was going to get my keys back from Ritter today, but...I'll talk to you later," Luce quickly changed direction before the emotions of the day could hit her full force.

"Everything okay?" Tyler asked as they left the building.

"Yes, sure." Everything would be, not far from now.

❧

"So, run that by me again," he said when they were sitting at a table in the diner across from the station. It was cozy enough, the food delicious, the setting a stark contrast to what they had to discuss. "One of those sign-wielding fellows is kidnapping women to keep them until they give birth? That's not only evil, but it's dangerous on so many levels. He's going to need supplies, food, medical. There's got to be a paper trail somewhere. Why would anyone go to those lengths?"

"They don't want to wait for the Supreme Court to rule their way?"

"I thought that had happened already."

"Sure, but they always want more. A federal ban. And they might get it."

The subject, omnipresent for the last few days, should have culled her appetite. Luce wasn't sure that anything could at this point. She wasn't feeling any guilt about the cheeseburger with fries either. There would be time for salad in the future.

"I get it, it's frustrating, but what you're suggesting...That's a stretch, Luce."

"Is it?"

Tyler regarded his own plate and sighed before he said, "It's not impossible, but I think we should be ready to consider a different angle. What if we're beating a dead horse here? That's not helping any of the women. You're letting this get to you."

Why would he say that?

"My private life has nothing to do with any of it."

Except it had. She got so angry that day when they didn't let her walk to the freaking front door in peace, angry at the men and women who were part of the group, and those who encouraged them. Judges, politicians, people like Hyde. There seemed to be no end to it, and it was much bigger than her own experience.

"I wasn't talking about your private life. All I'm saying is we don't have enough to go on."

"What is this?" she asked angrily. "Did Chomsky put you up to this? Or Troy? You seemed to get along pretty well the other day."

"I don't need anyone to tell me that you're on the verge of a burnout. I get it, Luce. I've been there. You've been after this Danes guy for a while. Your partner was shot today."

"Thanks for summarizing my day, but I was there. I know everything that happened. And it doesn't mean I'm wrong."

"It doesn't mean you're right."

She would have left there and then, but Luce decided the food was too good to abandon it. That, and she remembered she still owed him for the coffee they had earlier.

She wasn't ready to abandon the "theory," whatever the reason.

She still needed the evidence.

Chapter Eighteen

When Luce arrived at Kendra's, her host was still up, watching the news in her PJs. Luce was eager to share with Kendra her theory and the frustration she harbored for Tyler, hoping to find a sympathetic ear for both, but instead she stopped and took in the picture. She couldn't suppress the smile either.

"You had a good evening?" Kendra asked, diverting her attention from the TV screen.

"That depends." Luce stepped closer and sat next to her. Her initial eagerness to discuss her work progress with her was fleeting. Could it be that easy? What had she been afraid of all those months? "People keep blowing me off, but I think I have the right angle now. There's got to be something we've overlooked. I believe we can still bring those women home alive."

"I hope you're right."

She had expected a bit more enthusiasm. And questions maybe. Luce reminded herself that Kendra, too, had to be tired. Being confronted with the vitriol had rattled her, but Kendra was exposed to it on a daily basis.

"I hope so too. And I'm sorry. You have a lot on your plate, and maybe it's not the best time for me to be here. I swear there will be progress on the house too, sometime soon."

Kendra gave her a wry smile in return. She studied Luce for a moment long enough to turn uncomfortable.

"Are you sure you'll be okay to go back there? After what happened?"

"Nothing much happened," Luce said with a shrug. "I got startled, that's all."

"That's all?" She had the impression Kendra wanted to raise her voice. "You talk to Tyler about how you really feel about this?"

"What? Why would I? We work together, not by choice either. Feelings isn't really a subject that comes up. Why would you think that?"

"I don't know. You're right, maybe now's not a good time. You had a big day. It's good you finally found those girls. Is Ritter going to be okay?"

"Fortunately, yes." Luce wasn't sure how to deal with the sudden shift—but if Kendra wanted to talk about feelings, she would prove to her that she could, regardless of the long day. "I can't thank you enough for being so understanding. I'll make it up to you, I promise." When she leaned in, she hadn't expected Kendra to make space between them quickly. It served to both confuse and alarm her. "What's wrong?"

"Nothing. We should go to sleep."

"No, I think we should clear this up first. I swear that dinner was all about work. The food was great, but Tyler mostly got on my nerves because he's still lukewarm on my theory." When Kendra didn't answer, she added, "Is he the problem, or just any guy I've slept with?" Not that there had been that many. More than women, though. She hoped this wouldn't turn out to be an issue.

"You aren't accusing me of that, are you?" Kendra seemed equally shocked and appalled.

"No." She sighed, relieved, but the tension didn't leave her body entirely. "All of it, the case, being up close to those people, it's been messing with my mind. I know they think I should repent about something, but I won't apologize for anything. If there's anything I regret, it's that I didn't admit to myself earlier how I felt about you."

"I hear you. I swear. I just think we should take it slow. Not because you've had relationships with men, but because I'm not sure either one of us is ready for something serious."

Even though she kept the same warm tone, her words felt more like a slap to the face. More and more Luce could see how one mistake had led to a chain reaction. Without it? Who knew where she would be now? If there was one thing she knew for sure, it was that she couldn't stay.

"Okay. I guess I see your point," she said and got up from the couch.

"Luce! Where are you going?"

"Home. I thought we were on the same page, but don't worry. I'll give you time to figure it out."

"I didn't say never." Kendra jumped to her feet and followed her to the door. "Please. Could you just hear me out?"

At the door, Luce turned to her. She couldn't deal with her pleading gaze, all the implications, her own hopes and desires that might have been silly all along.

"Not tonight. I'm sorry. We'll talk another time."

⁂

Luce closed her front door behind her and locked, then she went from room to room. The CSU had finished up, but of course no one had bothered to clean up much, and the scrawling letters—*pig's blood*—still marred the wall.

She was too tired and dejected to deal with any of it. After tomorrow, she'd ask Chomsky for a couple of days off, just to fix the immediate damage and get the ball rolling on the renovations.

In her bedroom, she pushed the dresser in front of the door and put her gun on the bedside table. Just in case the person who considered her a murderer intended to come back for whatever "punishment" they seemed appropriate.

She couldn't figure out relationships to save her life, but if someone invaded her home again, she'd be ready.

✳

Luce made it to her desk before Lieutenant Chomsky came in. Coffee in hand and the bagel she'd bought on the way next to her computer, she breathed a sigh of relief at the relative peace.

She knew she was on to something. There was just one problem—Tyler and D.A. Troy had somewhat of a point.

She needed more to bolster that theory. Hard evidence. She had to be careful around people who were fairly good at playing and manipulating public opinion.

She had to make up her mind.

First of all, she had to clear said mind. Luce started organizing her notes, the findings on the victims, the suspects. Jared Hyde had admitted that some of the women had reacted angrily to him knocking on their doors, assuming they'd want to hear his talking points. She didn't think his ego would take it well.

Peters had doxxed patients, Hyde had access to addresses via his campaign. But how were either of them able to connect constituents to the clinic?

Kendra had been horrified to think one of her colleagues could leak information, but could she really vouch for everyone who had access to the files at one time or another?

Where was the missing link?

She checked her messages, realizing Dr. Martin had called her earlier. He didn't say what he wanted but asked her to call him back.

When she did, the receptionist told her that he was in with a patient. She'd have to get back to him later.

Next, she saw Lieutenant Chomsky arrive, doing a double-take when she saw Luce.

"Detective Allen. Don't you have a home? Okay, I'm sorry about that."

"Don't be. It's a fairly legit question, but I came here to clean up my desk some. Would you have a few minutes?"

"Of course. Let me get some coffee first."

No one but Luce understood this necessity of mornings and life better.

Five minutes later she sat in Chomsky's office, inexplicably nervous.

"You didn't get into another argument with the D.A.? " Chomsky prompted, her smile wavering when Luce didn't answer right away.

"No. No, it's not that. I'm going to need a bit of personal time. Not for long," she added quickly. "Just to make sure my home is all cleaned up, and I can put a few more security measures in place. I know it's not a great time, us being short-staffed right now."

"I'm sure we can make it work. If you could stay long enough to update everyone, and perhaps come in for a few hours for the rest of the week?"

So far so good.

"Yes. I'll do as much as I can today, and I'll be available for calls if anyone needs to check in. There's something else. I am convinced that whoever took these women planned it meticulously. And he wants to keep them until they give birth."

"That would indeed take a lot of preparation." At least she wasn't dismissing the idea right away.

"There has to be a paper trail somewhere, and I have an idea where to look. Hyde is getting a lot of donations, yet his campaign is bleeding money."

"Could be he's just bad at handling that money, but we can't ignore there are some arrows pointing back at him," Chomsky admitted. "What about the other suspect?"

"Peters might be helping him. Stalking the women, learning about their routines. Lieutenant, I need more resources on this. I know that sounds bad when I just asked you to give me time off, but I believe we can save these women."

"I'll see what I can do," Chomsky promised. "We'll have a quick briefing once Murphy and Troy are in, and then I'll need you to wrap up with Crayden and Meyers. I'm not taking you off the case completely, and I think your idea has merit," she added when Luce didn't keep a good enough poker face. "Either way, you can't be in two places at once."

How could she argue with that?

❦

As she imagined, Troy wasn't completely on board.

"I can't get you warrants based on a hunch," she said. "If, however, you have something solid, I'm all for taking a closer look."

Luce nodded, resigning to the fact that she wouldn't get any more of a concession from her.

"I'll join Crayden and Meyers for the rest of the day, but tomorrow, I'll only be here for a few hours in the afternoon. All my notes are on my desk, and...Rachel Benson works for an organization that did some fundraising for Cory Baldwin's group home. So, they might have known each other."

"Doesn't implicate Hyde, does it? Neither he nor Mr. Peters have any ties to that organization or the home?"

"Nothing that I could find so far," Luce admitted. Despite their haughty claims these men weren't much inclined to support the foster care system or couples who hoped to become parents.

"Okay." Troy didn't say anything more on the subject, but the small smile was enough to be irritating. "Back to Danes and the trafficking ring. Just so there won't be any surprises."

"There won't be. I can promise you that."

Chapter
Nineteen

Luce spent the afternoon with the other detectives wrapping up the interviews with two of Danes' associates that were willing to talk. Both claimed not to know about Joe Danes's whereabouts.

Dr. Martin didn't call again, so she decided to go see him in person, even given the risk that she might run into Kendra. Luce needed to apologize to her, again. Perhaps she had misunderstood her, too afraid that Kendra might close the door on something that hadn't even started yet? She might even manage to convey that yes, everything had gotten to her, the word "murder" still on her wall, the shouts as she walked to the entrance, seeing the rooms that had been a prison to Ashley Johnson and the others.

She might walk into something similar again. She might be wrong, and someone was kidnapping pregnant women for other twisted purposes.

Luce didn't see Tyler before she left that day, but she assumed they'd keep each other informed.

After seeing Dr. Martin, she'd get some paint and perhaps drop by Kendra's on her way home. She didn't want another night like the last one.

❧

It had started to rain lightly when she arrived at the Women's Health Center. A few holdouts in raincoats greeted her with the usual rhetoric. She was starting to get numb to it.

Once inside, she asked the receptionist to call Dr. Martin for her. He joined her a few minutes later.

"Detective Allen, it's good you're here. Come with me?"

"I was trying to reach you earlier. You left a message."

"Yes. It might be nothing, but I thought you might want to take a look at this."

He opened the door to his office and let her inside. "Please, have a seat."

Luce did as requested, and he opened a drawer in his desk and took out a couple of sheets.

"I'll have you know I'm not comfortable with this," he warned. "But if I'm right, not showing you this will be worse. You are aware of the amount of security we provide for staff and patients."

"Yes, I am."

"That's why this is so disturbing. This is a random list that was printed in my office. I didn't print it. And I'm worried that the person who left it behind might have done something inappropriate with it."

"May I?"

Still not the evidence Troy was asking for, but this was getting closer.

"When I saw what it was, I put it in a plastic sheath. You might still get prints off of it."

"That's...very considerate, thank you."

When Luce could finally take a look at the list, her jaw dropped.

The names of all the missing women were on it, including Wendy Tillis. Someone had compiled it from appointments in the past few weeks. Cory, Dawn, Rachel, about half a dozen she didn't know about, and...

Her own.

"Dr. Martin, I know you take confidentiality seriously, but you were right to call me. This is important. Three women on this list are missing. One is dead." She couldn't suppress the shudder. They had yet to determine what the intruder's intention had been. He had surprised her.

He could have killed her but ran instead.

Why?

"I have to take this to my colleagues. We need to warn those women."

"Of course." He sounded nervous now.

"I also need a list of anyone who has access to this office at any time. Please try to remember if there was any occasion that you might have forgotten to lock."

How did they pull it off?

Jared Hyde and Zach Peters were "regulars." They were familiar to the staff, so they couldn't just waltz in here and go through patients' files.

"I swear I haven't. I have no idea how they got in."

"Okay. I'll go back to the station. I'll also send you a technician to check if they left any traces behind."

This was...exciting for the lack of a better word. If she could solve this within the next twenty-four hours, everything in her life would change. Everything.

"I guess you have to do that."

"Don't worry, I'll make sure we have the paperwork, and we'll be discreet. Time is of the essence here."

"I understand."

"Could you wait here? I'll send someone right away."

She would. She also needed to warn the women whose appointments were coming up. Luce didn't think Chomsky would have any problem. This time, Troy would see the urgency.

Against all odds, she hoped all of it could happen without her own name ever being mentioned.

❧

At a red light, she called Tyler.

"Hey. I'm on my way out," he said. "Would you like to join me for dinner again? I swear I won't make you mad again."

"Listen, I need you to go back in and get Troy, or whoever can get us a warrant for Dr. Martin's computer. I just talked to him, and there's likely been a data breach. Whoever did it gained access to women's medical and contact information. We'll have to check if they left any prints behind, actual or digital ones."

"Wow, Luce, slow down. I'm going back up now. Chomsky is still upstairs. Do you want to talk to her?"

"I don't think that's necessary. I'll join you all when I'm there, and I can bring you up to speed at the same time."

"All right, I'll call Troy."

"Thank you. Tell her all the missing women's names are on the list, plus a few more. I'll be there in about twenty minutes."

"I'll see you then."

The rain had gotten heavier, reducing visibility to the point where she had to slow down. Fortunately, the traffic was lighter than usual, but Luce's impatience increased by the minute when she had to stop at another red light. Her findings were important, but she didn't think they justified using the siren.

"Come on," she muttered, tapping her fingers on the steering wheel.

There was an odd sound, or so she thought, coming from the left side. Luce's mind was on the missing women, then the apology she owed Kendra for running out on her.

The other vehicle hit the side of her car, the sudden brutal impact making the airbag deploy. The car teetered on two wheels for a brief moment before it came to a halt. All of it happened within seconds. Before she could fully process what had happened, the world went dark.

<hr>

"Something isn't right," Detective Murphy insisted. "She said she was only a few minutes away. Let me call her again."

Lieutenant Chomsky, too, had to agree that the recent developments were worrisome, especially when Murphy's call went to voicemail again.

"We need to get her in here, and we need those names," she said. "I'll head over to Dr. Martin's. You've been over there a few times. I want you to check the road. Keep in touch at all times."

"You want me to wait here?" Troy asked. If she was annoyed, she was polite enough not to show it.

"As a matter of fact, yes, Liz, I'd prefer if you could stay. I'll call you as soon as I learn anything new."

"I'll be in the break room."

"I'm sure we can resolve this quickly," she said while Murphy was already heading out.

Chomsky hoped her doubts wouldn't betray her. With what Luce Allen had told her earlier that day, it was fairly clear that she might have poked a hornet's nest. Call it a hunch, but

Chomsky didn't think that she'd stop for dinner somewhere after learning about this list. The sooner they got those names, the better.

"Lieutenant."

Murphy had already been halfway across the room when he came back and opened the door again, this time without knocking. He held his cell phone in his hand, his face ashen.

"There's been an accident."

"What happened?"

"Crash at an intersection. One of the cars was Luce's."

"How is she?" she asked, holding her breath.

"We don't know. The two vehicles are in the middle of an intersection, but there was no one when the uniforms arrived. She's gone, and so is the other driver."

"All right, call Dr. Martin. If he has the names, we need them now."

"You don't think..." Troy, who had returned, clutching a coffee as she stood in the doorway, didn't finish her sentence.

"We will pay both Hyde and Peters a visit," Chomsky clarified.

"What if Joe Danes—"

"Excuse me, Liz, but one of my detectives seems to be missing," she snapped at her. "Don't worry. I know how to do my job. Murphy?"

"On my way," he said.

⁂

Chomsky remembered her sage advice to Detective Allen, just a few hours prior, about not being able to be in two places at once. It seemed to be mocking her now. Officers had closed off the intersection around the two vehicles that both showed considerable damage.

One, stolen a few weeks ago. The other, Allen's RAV4. The driver's door was visibly damaged by the impact. The passenger's door stood wide open. The other driver might have been injured. She reasoned that a third person might have stood by. Whoever was behind this must have been planning it for a while, with considerable resources at their disposal.

She couldn't stay here, much as she wanted to oversee every single detail. She walked over to Detective Crayden. "Make sure they bring whatever they find straight to me. And find Ritter's file on the break-in."

Crayden nodded.

She cast one last look at the crash site, then got back into her car. Dr. Martin was on the way.

When she went to get Dr. Martin in the waiting area, he was accompanied by a woman who introduced herself as Dr. Kendra Jones.

"My colleague told me what happened, as it concerns my patients as well," she explained, and added after a small pause, "I'm also Detective Allen's friend. Luce has been staying with me since the break-in." Her stance made it clear that she wasn't going anywhere.

Chomsky made a judgment call. Dr. Jones' perspective could be helpful.

"Please, come with me."

She led them to the briefing room where Troy and Murphy were waiting for them. Introductions were made, though Murphy had met both doctors before.

"When I found that list, I called Detective Allen to get her opinion," he said. "I was reluctant to give out that information, but she convinced me that it was important."

"It sure is."

The tension in the room was palpable. Chomsky could sense that Murphy was a heartbeat away from shaking the man, his expression grim. She could sympathize, but she was also aware that privacy was at the very core of the work Dr. Martin and Dr. Jones did.

This was unorthodox, but Kendra Jones wasn't just Luce Allen's friend, but also Dr. Martin's colleague. She, too, had seen some of the patients that had been missing.

"Why didn't you tell me?" she asked him now, sounding irritated.

"I thought Detective Allen was going to get back to me. And she did! She was going to bring back the list, inform the other women and get a technician to my office. When they arrived, I thought everything was okay."

"Well, you can see it's not," Dr. Jones snapped.

"In any case, I brought you the names," Dr. Martin said, sounding uncomfortable. "This is the list I gave Detective Allen. I had made a copy in case this was ever important."

"Why is Luce's name on that list?" Murphy's question showcased the urgency once more, though his tone told Chomsky that this was a surprise to him more than to anyone else in the room.

She caught D.A. Troy's pensive gaze. Like herself, Jones and Martin seemed to hate every minute of this. They had to weigh their patients' privacy against their lives.

Chomsky despised having to expose the personal lives of anyone she worked with, but she might not have a choice this time.

Murphy's question sounded mostly rhetorical to her, but the break-in at Allen's house now had a context. She scolded herself for not connecting the dots earlier, not being more helpful. On the other hand, Luce Allen wasn't exactly someone who opened up to the people around her. Except Kendra Jones maybe.

"Fuck," he said when still no one had answered his question. Obviously, he had done the math. "She was right about them all along, wasn't she? This is why they broke into her house?"

"We still don't know who 'they' are exactly," Troy reminded him.

"We have eyes on Hyde and Peters," Chomsky said. This might not be for the doctors to hear, but they had been informed that nothing they learned could leave the room. If anyone understood the concept, it had to be them. "There were no prints other than Allen's and a few unidentified in the house. Peters' are on record."

"We have to bring him in. Hyde isn't going to crack."

"He called Peters a soldier. Let's find out how loyal he is," Chomsky concluded as she got to her feet.

"That's it?" Dr. Jones' eyes blazed with sudden anger and disbelief. "You asked us here to get our opinion, and now you're sending us away?"

"I'm sorry, Dr. Jones, there's nothing either one of you can do right now. Just let us do our work."

She hadn't expected any objections. Each person in the room knew exactly what was at stake.

Chapter Twenty

A t first glance, Luce thought she was in a hospital. As the room came into clearer view, she realized that it was a regular bedroom with white walls, sparsely furnished. A fraction of daylight came in from a window placed unreasonably high on the wall. She could see two doors, one left ajar leading to a bathroom, the other...likely locked.

Damn it.

She hurt all over, even though some of the pain was dulled. Shivers wracked her body despite the scratchy, musty-smelling blanket. Luce pushed it aside to reveal her bare legs, a bandage wrapped around one of them below her knee. She could see blood seeping through, the sight making nausea surge. Luce waited until the urge to throw up passed and carefully moved into a sitting position.

Wherever she was, she had to get out of here and fast. Even with her mind muddled by whatever drugs were in her system, she could guess that this was the location they'd been looking for since Wendy Tillis's body was found.

The perpetrator had made a "mistake" with Wendy when it came to the M.O. Luce didn't fit the profile either, but she reasoned she must have gotten too close for his comfort. If he planned to show her that she was right, letting her go was probably not high on his list of priorities.

Slowly, she managed to bring her legs over the edge of the bed. So far, better than expected. To no surprise, her phone or her pants were nowhere to be found. This would have to do, then. Luce pushed herself off of the bed.

Unable to hold in the undignified sound when she put weight on her injured leg, she nearly ended up face-first on the floor, the water shooting to her eyes.

Not just because of the pain. Anger, a moment of unadulterated fear, for herself, and for the women she suspected were held in the same place by...who? A couple of egomaniacal men? There had to be a way. Sadly, at this moment, she had no idea what it was.

She should have called her mother more often. Jill. Talked to Kendra before engaging in a familiar pattern of denial.

It was a little too late for any of it. Tears wouldn't help her.

She needed to do better.

She needed a plan.

⁓

In the morning, the head of the department's lab had confirmed that Dr. Martin's computer had been hacked into from the office of a group called The Defenders of Life.

Murphy had come in early and was now in the interview room with a gloating Peters. Chomsky had stayed in the observation area. It wasn't that she didn't trust him, but this wasn't something she felt comfortable delegating.

"Some of their members join us, but I'm still not a part of them."

"No? Who are you working for, then?"

"Working?" He gave a contemptuous laugh, and Chomsky held her breath.

Murphy knew she was watching him. He'd do this by the book, especially now that another cop's life was on the line. It wasn't hard to tell he was tempted to throw out the book. None of them had gotten any sleep in the last few hours.

"This is what we believe in," Peters went on. "Saving lives. You should try it sometime."

He had threatened Allen, but he wasn't going to give away much.

"Lieutenant?"

She turned to see Detective Crayden standing in front of her.

"There's a Maggie Rowland here. She wants to talk to Detective Allen."

Chomsky cast another glance at the room where Murphy and Peters were engaged in a stand-off.

"Let's see what she has to say."

❧

Luce had managed to stand, but not more than that. When she heard the footsteps coming closer, she sat back down on the edge of the bed, and on second thought, pulled the blanket over her legs. A key was turned in the lock, and the door opened to reveal her captor.

His identity? Not a surprise at this point.

"I see you're awake, good. We can finally talk."

Instinctively, she shrank away, though Hyde remained leaning against the door. A smug smile played over his face which no doubt had to do with the gun he was carrying in a hip holster.

"Really? I gave you many chances to talk."

"Come on, Detective, you're smarter than that. I couldn't let you jeopardize the important work that I do."

"Abducting women? Killing them?"

"Maybe not that smart," he scoffed.

Add insult to injury, why don't you, asshole?

"Enlighten me, then. You don't seem to care about the life of the mother."

"I care that they're *carrying* a life. Wendy ran. You can imagine I've updated security since that unfortunate incident."

Luce knew she had to make careful use of her energy. She couldn't keep up what she'd been doing for weeks, react to every outrageous, ignorant or bizarre statement—like calling a woman's death an unfortunate incident. Let him think he was the smart one.

"So, it's true. You're forcing women to give birth in this...What even is this? A makeshift cult of one?"

Hyde laughed. "This, detective, is the future. Since you've been so desperately trying to solve the riddle, I thought why not show you how it works. Maybe you'll even understand."

She gazed at the blanket covering her legs, wishing she had her pants.

"You understand that in order for those babies to be healthy, the mothers need to be healthy as well. You give them food?"

He shook his head as if she had said something stupid.

Luce's mind was still reeling with the implications. Were there infants in this house? What was he doing with them?

"Of course I give them food. Unfortunately, you figured out correctly that my campaign is in a bit of financial trouble. It's not cheap to stand up for your principles. We're lucky Rachel is an excellent cook, and she still has quite some time to go. Perhaps you could replace her."

*But I am not...*Even finishing the thought seemed too much of a risk. Luce didn't want to give him any reminder. He wanted her to cook a meal, she could bide her time until she could assess the situation and engage the other women in...what? Escape? If they were all in the same room, they could overpower him?

So many ifs.

"I can cook a decent meal," she said.

"I'm so glad. I have a couple of them in the morning sickness phase. And of course you have a lot to make up for."

"For my beliefs? For wanting to help these women? Isn't that what you claim you do?"

He laughed, brushing his finger over the handle of the gun.

"I don't punish people for their thoughts, wicked as they might be. You forgot that I know. I've known since you first made me come to the station that you had murdered your baby."

He was studying her with interest, to gauge the effect his words had, Luce assumed. They loved the shock value of those talking points, and it worked with too many people, still.

She wasn't going to let him bait her.

"You have nothing to say? Perhaps I should introduce you to Rachel. She saw the light quickly, and now things are so much easier. Of course, she was still expecting when she came here."

"You mean when you abducted her." *Careful, Luce*.

"Semantics."

"What about Cory? You weren't driving that car, were you?"

"No," he admitted. "Sweet Cory. In cases like hers, soldiers can be useful. But if your colleagues ever find him, he won't be of much use. He doesn't know anything except a fake name and a combination of numbers to get paid. The Defenders are stealthy that way."

"That's interesting. You got Maggie to do your dirty work too?"

"Maggie, no. She didn't quite have the skills required for our mission. But enough about this. We should be talking about you."

She shifted slightly and winced. It was clear that whatever drugs she'd been given were wearing off.

"You got into the patients' files. You know my history. What else is there to know?"

"Oh, I'm always interested in the why before we can proceed, especially with a case where I was sadly too late. You have a job with good benefits, a house, and even though no one seems to like you much, some family not too far. You had no reason."

He had a gun. She could barely stand, let alone attack him without a plan. Those were the only reasons Luce kept silent. She'd heard the old, tired arguments in person and seen them online, from people, who would never acknowledge that her decision had been none of their business. Who wouldn't lift a finger to house and feed all the babies they wanted to be born.

She wouldn't succeed in explaining this to a man who had abducted several women to interfere with said decision and had casually accepted the death of one.

"You want me to have remorse," she stated. "Do you have any remorse about Wendy?"

"Wendy would have been fine if she'd stayed here. I am not a murderer."

"She would still be alive if it wasn't for you." Luce couldn't help it, not with the truth this obvious.

"I am a good person!" he yelled, his change of demeanor somewhat expected but still sudden enough it made her flinch. "I haven't killed anyone." He spun around, about to open the door, but turned to her again. "I'll be right back. Don't try anything, or I swear, it won't end well for the others."

When he was gone, Luce pushed back the blanket once more, not surprised when more blood had stained the bandage. She was in deep trouble, and she didn't exactly have a history of relying on those closest to her.

She would need to find a way to get past that pain, and quick.

❧

He returned a few minutes later. After unlocking the door, he first let in the woman carrying a tray. Hyde was training the gun on her.

Rachel Benson held her head up high despite the humiliation. She was wearing a white T-shirt and grey sweatpants and shoes.

Her stomach rumbled at the sight of a bowl of soup, a slice of bread and an apple. It had to be later than she'd thought. She sought Rachel's gaze, but the other woman looked straight ahead.

"Isn't she great?" Hyde was back to the jovial tone and smile. "Such invaluable help. I wouldn't know what to do without her. Isn't that right, Rachel?"

"I'm so glad."

Luce searched for a hint of sarcasm. She couldn't find any. Was he drugging the others too?

How could she make contact? Before she could come up with any idea, Hyde said, "Remember, I was telling you about Luce? She's a cop. I'm sure she's been imagining how she'll bring you all back, but we all know that won't happen now. First of all, look at her, she's in no shape to jeopardize what we're doing here. And you don't want to leave, do you?"

"I am good," Rachel said in the same hollow tone, though her eyes flickered to Luce, holding her gaze for a heartbeat.

"You hear that, Luce? Now eat. We'll take a look at your leg later."

Apparently, he wasn't feeling any remorse for that either, not that she had expected it.

She had been plunged into a horror movie, part *The Handmaid's Tale*, part *Silence of the Lambs*.

There had to be a way out.

"Thanks for the soup," she said. His smile deepened, while Rachel Benson gave an almost imperceptible nod.

Chapter
Twenty-One

E ither her meal was really that good, or she hadn't had food for longer than she thought. While she ate the soup using the plastic spoon that was part of a children's set, Luce examined the room. Visually only, at this point. Four white walls. A window that was too high and too narrow to be of any use.

The door. An old-fashioned lock and key. There was no source of light other than that window, so at some point she'd be in the dark. Luce paused, reminded of the Danes cousins and their underground maze. Twisted minds thinking alike.

She couldn't go there now, or she'd risk getting lost in the details and images Ashley had evoked with her statement.

"You're done, good." Hyde came close enough to whisper to her. "I don't doubt you could do something with that baby spoon if you wanted to, but we'll make sure Rachel doesn't leave anything behind, right?"

The other woman, who had been quietly standing in a corner, stiffened but obediently put dishes and utensils back onto the tray. She had brought a bag with her that contained another bandage, wipes and anti-bacterial cream.

"Let's take care of this quick. We have more work to do."

Rachel wasn't in the medical profession. Luce hated that he made her do any of it.

"I can change that bandage myself," she said.

"But she is happy to do it, aren't you, Rachel?"

What she hated more was being such a disappointment, to herself, to the others. She was supposed to save them, damn it!

Luce bit her lip when Rachel carefully removed the old bandage, feeling her vision gray out at the sight.

She could not faint, in front of him, or the woman she needed to trust her.

Luce avoided it just barely.

❦

The gun first. Then the keys.

Luce was startled to realize she'd nodded off while alternately trying to fight the pain and wracking her brain in search of a solution. Hyde might even mean it when he said murdering the women wasn't his intention. That might buy her some time.

It didn't mean she could wait for her colleagues to find her. Luce knew firsthand that this location had to be well hidden if he could maintain his twisted idea for weeks. And there was no doubt something twisted was going on.

He had known that Wendy wanted to be a mother—he had held her against her will anyway.

In all those conversations they'd had before, Luce had, without meaning to, given him an insight into how to get to her: She had no doubt he had brought her here to show off his efforts, knowing it was killing her not being able to help.

He was underestimating her.

While the sunlight was fading outside, Luce tried to stand once more, keeping one hand on the nightstand to support herself. Her eyes welled up again, but she didn't faint or throw up.

The place had to be well insulated, because she couldn't hear any sounds that indicated the presence of another person. In fact, it was eerily quiet, the thought making her shudder. That's what he expected of them. To be quiet, obedient.

He wasn't going to get that from her.

Rachel Benson, too, was biding her time. Or maybe that was just her own wishful thinking, and Hyde had created his own dystopia?

It had been a while since that soup and apple, hunger making her light-headed.

Luce made it across the room to the bathroom that barely fit the toilet and tiny sink. A soap dispenser on the wall.

She pulled hard, not achieving anything though she almost lost her balance. She didn't find anything that could be used as a weapon. The lid of the toilet tank wasn't coming off. One towel.

She made her way back out, disgusted by what she'd seen. She hoped the setup was more comfortable for the other women, but she doubted it.

Luce sat on the edge of the bed, catching her breath. The new bandage still looked clean. She ached all over, but as far as she could tell, she'd been lucky. The results of the crash could have been much worse.

She flexed her fingers, making a fist. Even if he put down the gun at some point, going at him would be risky.

If she could get to a phone...Preferably her own. This would all be over within minutes.

She might be fooling herself, but she had to psych herself up for that confrontation. It was the only chance.

To her surprise, Hyde returned before it was dark. This time, he had Rachel serve wine in a plastic cup.

"You're kidding me, right? What did you put in it?"

"Always expecting the worst of people, aren't you? I would invite Rachel to stay with us, but as you can imagine, she can't have alcohol. There's no danger for you, but I thought you might appreciate it."

"For what?"

"Your leg is still hurting, I assume? Let me just walk Rachel back to her room, and I'll be right with you. Then we can talk."

Luce didn't have a lot of time. She picked up the cup and smelled the contents—her senses told her red wine. She was fairly certain that it contained drugs. If she threw it on him, would it be enough to distract him?

"There you are," he said as if she had the option of going anywhere in the meantime. "Really, I would drink it if I were you."

"So, you want to make conversation? You hacked my medical file. Don't you know everything already?"

He sat at the foot of the bed, gun in one hand, an identical cup in the other.

"Lucinda Allen. Not close to anybody, family, or even the ones you call friends. Lied to the father of her baby...why? He would have insisted you do the right thing?"

"There was no baby, and I didn't lie. Neither of us had an interest in starting a family together."

"You are always so angry, Luce. I wonder why that is. Isn't there something missing from your life?"

Fuck you. It was on the tip of her tongue, but he'd just see it as confirmation. She wasn't going to give him anything else.

"I guess you'll tell me."

"I think you're sad. I care about you."

She nearly snorted.

"I care about all of you. It's too bad you can't see that yet. I can only imagine that in your mind, I brought you here to punish you, because you have this idea of saving them, and now you feel like a failure."

He was trying to get to her. Luce recognized every trick. She wasn't sad or feeling guilty though she knew there were people she'd call more often once this was over.

"The good news it that you don't have to do anything, except understand that they don't need saving, not from you. Now don't be silly and enjoy the wine. It wasn't cheap."

How was that her problem?

She took a small sip, surprised to realize that he had to be telling the truth—the quality was noticeable even to someone who rarely drank. Definitely not her problem.

"So, what is it for? What have I done to deserve it?" It sounded only marginally sarcastic."

"Nine months is a long time," he said and took a big gulp of his own cup. "I thought one last time wouldn't harm. You still don't get it?"

Her fingers tightened around the handle as he put the gun next to him. So damn cocky.

Hyde let out an angry curse when the steak knife Rachel had smuggled in broke his skin, sinking into his shoulder. It had been a matter of a split-second when she slipped it under the pillow while collecting the tray with Luce's dishes. Luce had no idea how Rachel had managed to get it, and she had no time to wonder.

She used the small window she had to get to her feet, lack of shoes and pants be damned, and get to the gun. Her leg was burning, but she was standing, and she was going to get out of this room.

Her angle had been slightly off she realized when he pulled out the knife and tossed it aside.

"Stay away!" she warned, raising the gun.

"What do you think this is?"

When he charged at her, she pulled the trigger, only to be left with a dissatisfying sound as he slammed her against the door.

"You'd think I'd keep a loaded gun in a house full of pregnant women?"

He tried to wrestle it from her, both of them toppling to the ground. She managed to hold on to it and slam it into his face, his grip finally loosening. Luce hit him another time, just so she could get free and stand up. Hyde was still conscious but barely, his lids fluttering as he uttered a pitiful moan.

Luce went as fast as she was physically able to, took the keys from him, got out of the room and locked the door from the outside. She could see stars dancing in front of her eyes, but she couldn't slow down now.

Down the hall were several doors. Luce knocked on the first one. "Rachel? Cory?"

"It's locked. Can you get in?" she heard Rachel's voice.

Luce tried the key, sighing in relief when she realized it had to fit all the doors.

Inside the room, slightly bigger than the one she had escaped from, Luce was faced with another problem: Rachel was cuffed to the bed frame.

She suppressed a curse. The knife would have been helpful.

"Okay. I'll try to find some sort of tool after I get to a phone, okay?"

For the first time, she could see emotion flicker over Rachel's face. "Hurry up, please?"

"I will," she promised. "I'll be right back."

Chapter Twenty-Two

L uce turned on lights on her way as she unlocked another door. She instantly recognized Cory Baldwin. The teenage girl stared back at her in shocked disbelief, which might have been because she expected Hyde, or because of the fact that Luce still wasn't wearing pants. Cory was wearing gray sweatpants and a white t-shirt, the same as Rachel.

A prison uniform. She, too, was cuffed to the bed.

"Cory, my name is Luce Allen. I'm with the police. I'm going to get you out of here."

"He said it would be too late for me." Fresh tears spilled over her cheeks. "Can you really get us out?" So, she was aware of the others too.

She had to go faster.

"I have to find a phone and call my colleagues. Are you hurt?"

"The man...he twisted my shoulder when he pulled me into the van. I'm scared. Please don't leave me!"

Luce realized that she was the first friendly face Cory had seen since she was taken. She could only guess how Hyde must have berated her.

"I'll be quick. He's locked in right now."

"Really?"

"I swear. We'll all go home today. I promise you."

Cory nodded, and Luce had no choice but to continue on her quest.

At the end of the hallway, the door to a kitchen stood open. She inspected it quickly, choosing a couple of tools that would hopefully help her open the cuffs. No phone. Luce was about to take the stairs leading to an upper level of the building when the scream stopped her.

She ran right back to open the door, stopping cold at the sight. This room was slightly bigger than the others. One of the women, she could tell, was in need of immediate medical attention, blood staining the sheets underneath her.

The other one was Dawn Moreno.

Luce didn't take the time to introduce herself but went straight to try the screwdriver on the cuff's lock to free the distraught woman who was barely conscious, and then Dawn.

"Ms. Moreno. What happened to her?"

"I'm not sure. She was already here when I arrived," Dawn said, a shudder wracking her body. "It's not time for her yet."

Luce had an idea of what Hyde was trying to achieve, but the reality of it still stunned her, even more warped and cruel than she could have imagined.

"Could you get upstairs, try to find a phone and call 911? I'm going to get the others."

"What did he do to you?" Dawn asked, her gaze sliding from Luce's face to her bare legs.

"Not important right now. Please, go. I locked him in my room," she said when Dawn was still hesitating. "He can't get out. We need to get her to a hospital."

Dawn nodded and left. Socks, no shoes on any of them.

Luce suppressed a curse when all she found in the adjacent bathroom was a couple of those small hand towels. She held one under the faucet and turned on the cold water, then went to wipe the woman's forehead.

"What's your name?" she asked.

"Layla," the woman answered. She sounded short of breath. "I don't want to die."

"You won't. He won't win. Help will be here soon." Luce hated to leave her alone even for a second, but there was strength in numbers, and she had a bad feeling knowing Rachel and Cory were still tied to their beds. "Just let me get the others, okay? They're just in the next room."

She went to Cory first who was shaking and crying.

"It's okay. We will all leave soon, all right?" She hoped Dawn had managed to find a phone. Layla couldn't wait much longer.

"So, you had use for that knife," Rachel said, a hint of satisfaction to her tone when she finally stood, rubbing her wrists.

"I'll tell you about it later. Let's go. You've seen Layla?"

"I have." Rachel's expression was grim.

"Something's not right. Dawn is looking for a phone, but we have to take care of her first."

Rachel and Cory followed her. Luce could tell that Rachel had doubts.

"I will stay with her," she said. "You should all get upstairs, wait there for the police." There was no way Layla could walk, and assessing the situation, Luce had changed her mind on keeping all of them in the same room. For the time being, Hyde couldn't get out. She didn't want any of them become more traumatized than they already were, in case Layla took a turn for the worse.

"I'll stay here too."

Luce gave Rachel a sharp look, but the other woman's gaze was daring her.

"You should go."

"You're hurt too," Rachel pointed out.

Realizing there wasn't any point in arguing, Luce turned to Cory. "All right, you go find Dawn and wait for the police."

"Yes, Ma'am." The teenager was quick to oblige.

When she had left, Luce turned to Layla whose breathing was a bit less ragged.

"How is the pain?"

"Not as bad as before."

"I think she's going into labor," Rachel commented. "They better find that phone soon." She all but whispered the second part.

He had to have medical supplies somewhere, fresh sheets, something to make sure his plan could work...or perhaps Hyde had done a job preparing for this as shoddily as he ran his campaign.

"Did he ever show you some sort of supply closet?"

"What do you mean? How long do you think this will take?"

Luce pulled her aside as Layla closed her eyes.

"We've been searching for this place for weeks. Once Dawn and Cory find that phone and call 911, they're going to trace it."

"That might take a while?"

"We have to work with what we've got."

"He's not exactly a big spender," Rachel said with disdain. "I think I could find you some pants though."

"That would be helpful," Luce admitted. "Maybe another blanket or something?"

"On it," Rachel promised, and just like that, Luce was alone with a woman who still might die, and her own fears.

She took Layla's hand, heartened by Layla squeezing hers in a fairly strong grip.

Minutes passed by.

She would have liked to do everything. Chomsky's words about not being able to be in two places at once came to mind.

Layla was the only one of the women who couldn't walk out on her own. It wasn't really a choice.

They'd find a phone.

Her colleagues would find them.

When Layla drew a shocked breath, Luce looked up, almost thinking they were sharing a hallucination.

Reality was worse than that. Leaning heavily on the doorframe, still bleeding from the wound in his shoulder, stood Jared Hyde.

"You shouldn't have done that, Luce," he sneered. "I already knew you were going to Hell, but now you'll get there sooner."

She held out her hands in front of him.

"Why don't we leave this place? Layla here needs help. I'll come with you. I promise."

"Lying bitch!"

"I mean it. You know I'm telling the truth. All I ever wanted was to free these women. Layla has done nothing wrong. She deserves a chance."

"She deserves nothing! Neither do you."

When he closed the distance between them, she ducked. Not wasting any time, Luce got a couple of punches in before he kicked her leg, knocking the breath out of her. His hands were around her neck, squeezing...

Until he dropped to the floor with a pained yelp. Luce coughed, trying to get enough air into her lungs. The image of Rachel holding the folding chair in a white-knuckled grip wavered and disappeared for a heartbeat.

The pained moan from behind her reminded her she couldn't let her guard down yet.

Rachel pulled a set of cuffs from the pocket of her sweatpants. "You want to do the honors?" she said. "Make it official."

"You bet."

Hyde was barely conscious, but enough to keep hurling slurs at them. Luce took the time to search his pockets and found the knife he had obviously used on the lock, before she put the cuffs on him.

"Jared Hyde, you are under arrest..."

She made it all the way through the Miranda warning before Layla screamed.

Chapter Twenty-Three

Despite her best efforts to remain alert and conscious, Luce was missing a period of time, she realized when she found herself face to face with a paramedic, and an alarmed looking Tyler. He removed his hand from her shoulder as if sensing that she needed to moment to orient herself.

They were still surrounded by hectic activity, but as she looked around, neither Layla nor Hyde were in the room any longer. She took a deep breath, her vision starting to gray out again. This time, she held on to consciousness.

"She's going to make it, right?"

"I'm sure." Tyler's tone and expression told her he was anything but sure.

"You're getting all of them to the hospital first? Has anyone called the group home?"

"We're taking care of it," he promised. "Now let's get you checked out."

She was cold, still in pain, feeling nauseated. None of it mattered, knowing that Hyde's sick idea had come to an end. Luce realized she was still sitting on the floor leaning against the bed, not the blood-stained one, but the second one she'd retreated to at some point to give the incoming medical and law enforcement personnel room. She remembered an officer talking to her and then...nothing.

Nothing was a tempting prospect, if only for a little while.

"I can walk," she said, pushing herself up from the floor only to have her injured leg fold underneath her. The paramedic was faster.

"Maybe you could, but we don't want to take any chances." Her voice, too, was suspiciously kind.

"I'll come with you."

Luce wondered what he was thinking. The crash. The lack of pants—Rachel had never made it to that supply closet. Given the context, there was no way he hadn't learned the whole story. Her name was on the list.

She gritted her teeth against the flare of pain when the paramedic helped her onto the gurney and then closed her eyes.

To her relief, Tyler couldn't stay long. Luce had no illusions—he'd be back with more questions, and some might be of a more private nature.

On the bright side, her leg wasn't broken, just badly bruised and cut in places. She wouldn't need a cast, but that hot bath she'd been craving would have to wait a little longer. She'd nearly cried when the doctor told her.

She only had a few minutes to herself, after staff, Tyler, and Lieutenant Chomsky who had dropped by, left her alone.

Even though exhaustion had settled into her bones, she couldn't sleep, her mind frantic with the experiences and dire possibilities of the recent hours.

When the door opened again, Luce almost thought she was hallucinating when Kendra walked in.

"Hey." She closed the distance between them quickly and leaned down to greet Luce with a gentle kiss on the cheek.

"I'm so happy to see you. How are you?"

"Still can't take that damn hot bath." Her eyes were welling up again. How embarrassing was that?

"You can stay with me for a while. I'm taking a couple of weeks off."

"Because of me? You shouldn't. I don't think I'll be off work that long..." Kendra did have a point, she realized. After the physical part, she'd have to see the department psychiatrist to prove she was still able to do the job.

With a sigh, Luce sank back into the pillow.

"Okay, probably I will. Do you know anything about the others?"

"Layla is alive. But it was much too early. She miscarried."

Kendra squeezed her hand gently.

Luce nodded, unwilling to examine the wave of emotion. She had been held hostage by a psychopath who had willingly jeopardized the lives of women. She felt entitled to be emotional.

"You saved them, Luce. They didn't tell me everything, but I heard enough."

"I didn't do that much."

"I know quite a few people who would disagree, and I'm one of them. You brought them home, and because of you, the other patients on the list could be warned." Kendra's eyes, too, were bright with unshed tears. "I was so afraid."

"I'm sorry."

"This wasn't your fault."

Luce had given the question a lot of thought. Perhaps, if she hadn't been on collision course with everyone around her, they would have bought into her theory sooner? She couldn't turn back time. And she knew that Kendra had believed her all along.

"Thank you," she said.

Kendra sat on the side of the bed, and Luce leaned into her embrace, more grateful than ever for her steadfast presence.

"None of this changed my mind," she felt the need to say.

"I know. You need to stay angry. I need to focus on what matters most."

In this moment of relative privacy, it occurred to Luce that this had always been a good combination. They were.

Kendra stayed until she fell asleep.

Tyler arrived the next morning while she was having breakfast.

"How's it going?" he asked.

"Up. Not yet running. Breakfast isn't half bad, but maybe that's because soup and an apple was all that the cheap asshole had to offer." Luce shook her head, her stomach churning at the memory. "I can't even imagine...He held them there for weeks. Do you know how Wendy got away?"

"Not yet. We are compiling the women's statements. It's a horror story. You were right all along." His tone was pained. She wasn't the only one asking herself what she could have done differently, to free the women sooner.

"I'm afraid there's not a lot I can add to what I told you already. I wasn't sure I was going to make it, but I knew I had to try." Luce didn't care to put into words her anger and fear of what might have happened, both occupying her mind. She remembered repeating Hyde's words to her yesterday, still in a bit of a fog. That fog was clearing. It made her want to break something. "Rachel was amazing, hitting him over the head with that chair."

"So were you. First thing the fucker did was get in touch with his lawyer and tell everyone you assaulted him."

"What?"

"Relax. That is obviously going nowhere," Tyler hurried to add. "He might claim he didn't want to kill anyone, but Wendy Tillis died, and Layla Dorman likely wouldn't have made it if it wasn't for you."

Last night, when Kendra had held her hand until she fell asleep, Luce had imagined she could be moving on from this quickly, go on with life which would be new and improved. With Kendra. And finished home improvements.

Today, all she felt was raw, that beautiful future not yet within reach.

"Why didn't you tell me?"

Their timing had always been awful, and this was no exception.

"Why would I? We had a couple of one-night-stands. There was never anything else in the picture."

"Maybe not."

Luce didn't like the vagueness of his answer, but she wasn't going to pursue the subject, hoping he'd feel the same.

"I understand this was your choice to make, but I still would have liked to know. Would that have been too much to ask? I wouldn't have tried to change your mind, but I could have come with you. Maybe..."

She shook her head, not wanting to hear the rest. What she had told Kendra was the truth—there was no other way for the story to end. "You came here to be closer to your family...and perhaps, Susan. But regardless, we were never going to be together. I am not a mother. No one will decide that for me."

"Sure. I get all that."

"Do you?"

"I do. Just remember sometime that there are people in your corner. You don't have to do it all by yourself..." He sighed when she didn't react. "I guess we're done here for the moment."

"That's good. She needs her rest." Kendra, who had entered the room, spoke with the authority of a doctor who actually worked here, even though she did not. Luce almost smiled. She appreciated that Tyler hadn't made their conversation unnecessarily complicated, but the recent hours had taken a toll, nonetheless. She did need rest. And Kendra.

"Dr. Jones. I'll see you, Luce," Tyler said curtly before he left.

"That was surprisingly easy," Kendra commented.

It was also the end of the line.

Kendra quietly moved the tray out of the way and pulled her close. Nothing was easy at the moment, but perhaps, someday in the future, it could be again.

Chapter
Twenty-Four

E veryone returned to their respective workplaces, Kendra, to prepare for her two-week, sort of vacation, Tyler, to wrap up loose ends. Luce wished she could be present for the latter, though she was equally grateful she didn't have to be in the same room with Hyde at this time.

He, too, had been treated for injuries, all of which, she thought grimly, he deserved. Not that it could ever make up for what he'd done to his victims.

She took a deep breath, aware that she wasn't ready yet to acknowledge that this didn't just include the other women anymore, that it had gone far beyond a case.

When the nurse came by, he provided her with the paper and pen she had asked him for earlier.

"Thank you. I know that's not exactly in your job description."

"No problem."

"And those release papers...?"

"Probably this afternoon, but I'll check with the doctor."

When she was alone again, Luce jotted down a few notes. She didn't have any more excuses to delay those conversations with the contractor, and she would have to think about budget and limits of the plans.

Another thing on the list...No, she wasn't going to put that off any longer. Luce picked up her phone and called Jill.

She caught her a few minutes before a meeting.

"I'm sorry, I didn't mean to disturb you..."

"Are you okay?"

She didn't mean to go into depth on that subject either, but apparently her tone was still giving her away.

"Mostly," she ascertained. "The last few days were a bit...rough. I'm still living on a construction site, but I'll put a rush on the renos. Once it's done, you and Josie could come for a weekend sometime. We could do a bit of sightseeing around town."

"I'd love that," Jill said, sounding surprised. Luce didn't blame her.

"Maybe I'll call my mom and we'll all have dinner? She'd love to see Josie too."

She would have to call her mother soon. She wasn't sure how much national press Hyde's case would get.

"That sounds great. I'm sorry, I really have to get to this meeting. I'll call you back later?"

"Sure. I look forward to it."

First steps. Luce would call her mother when she was sure she could talk to her without revealing too much.

She wrote *Kendra – restaurant (real date!)* on her list, resisting the urge to draw a heart. If it was silly, who cared? It was exactly what she needed right now, to find her way back to what was real, and important.

❦

"Ready?"

The door opening nearly made her jump out of her skin, but at the sight of Kendra, her heartbeat calmed.

"That depends. I have my papers, the test results are encouraging...Did you really take two weeks off, or did I dream that?"

"Oh, I did." Kendra smiled gently. "If someone doesn't intervene, that house of yours will never be done. Two weeks should be okay to light a fire under those people—or find a new firm if you prefer."

"That is...I don't know what to say. Thank you so much. Let's get out of here."

"Your chariot awaits, Ma'am," the nurse from earlier said behind Kendra.

"Oh no. I can walk."

The words found an echo somewhere in her mind, making her queasy for a few seconds. Luce changed her mind quickly, before he said, "Sorry about that. Hospital policy."

"It's also faster that way," Kendra added. "You appreciate that, right?"

"Can't do anything about it with the two of you ganging up on me, but yes, I appreciate that."

As he wheeled her along the hallways to the elevators, pushing the button to go several floors down, Luce had to admit they had a point.

Kendra had parked at the entrance. The few steps to the car were enough of a challenge for today. Luce gritted her teeth as she fastened her seatbelt, then she leaned forward to cover her face with her hands.

"What's wrong?"

"Oh, I have no idea where to start. My car. The asshole hit my car—not Hyde, but someone he paid. I'm not sure what my insurance will do with that."

"One thing at a time," Kendra reminded her. "I'd like you to think about what you want for dinner. I promise that's all you need to do today."

"That's...kind. Thank you."

They shared a smile, both knowing that Luce's mind would be on various things, many of which had to do with work.

"I'll do that. I swear. But I need to talk to Tyler. And I'd really love a shower, wash my hair."

"Okay, three things. But that's the limit."

"I promise."

Kendra took her hand again for a few seconds before she started the car.

"Let's go home."

Home. The term was starting to gain a whole different meaning—or perhaps Luce had ignored the obvious for a long time.

"Thank you," she whispered again, not quite ready to put different words to her all-over-the-place emotions.

"You're welcome."

<hr />

It wasn't until they arrived at Kendra's home that Luce learned how much she had gone out of her way to make Luce feel welcome.

"Okay, we'll get to that shower in a bit. When you have decided what to eat, I'll take care of that, and you can talk to Tyler? Before I forget, these are yours." She took a set of keys out of her purse and laid them on the table.

"The ones I gave to Ritter. How...?"

"I did a bit of meddling," Kendra admitted. "I paid him a quick visit and asked him, and he made sure they gave them to me so I could get you some clothes. I thought you might be more comfortable."

Luce didn't know what to say without sounding like a broken record. "You're amazing. Thank you so much."

"You might have heard that your lieutenant called me and Dr. Martin in. I used every bit of leverage I had, but I didn't have to work that hard. They care."

"I should have checked in on Ritter." Guilty conscience was starting to creep up on her.

"He's aware of why you didn't. And he wishes you well. Anyway. You'd like that shower now?"

Kendra sounded a bit too chipper on the last few words, indicating she might be nearly as nervous as Luce was.

"This was not how I wanted to get naked with you," Luce admitted.

"I'll be honest. I had different ideas too. But there will be time for them."

She leaned in to kiss Luce, softly, on the lips.

It had to be true.

Chapter Twenty-Five

L ater, she was comfortably settled on the couch with a pile of takeout menus, seemingly from every restaurant in the city. Luce was glad that Kendra had been able to put aside whatever was developing between them in favor of her warm, empathetic but somewhat detached doctor persona.

She hadn't imagined that getting out of her clothes, being confronted with the bruises, would make it all come rushing in: From the crash, to the white room, trying to find a way out of a physical prison, and the one created by his delusions. Luce hadn't realized how cold she'd been all of the time. Vulnerable.

Kendra had packed a pair of sweats, but they reminded her too much of the "uniform" Hyde had put together for his hostages. This was why she sat on Kendra's couch in slacks and a top she might have worn for a date out.

Better. Not great.

Having to make a decision on dinner was near overwhelming. "Okay."

Kendra gently took the menu from her hands. Heat rose to her face when Luce realized she was trembling.

"I can take care of it. Why don't you call Tyler tomorrow?"

"I'd rather get it over with. You order whatever you like. After those couple of days, what they served at the hospital was like gourmet food, so...It'll be okay."

"No problem. I think I have an idea."

Kendra went to the kitchen to give her some privacy.

"Hey, Tyler," she said when he picked up. "Luce here. Where are we on Hyde and Peters?"

"Progressing. How are you?"

"Progressing," she said, and they shared a hesitant laugh.

"All right. Peters did abduct Cory Baldwin, and he's quite proud of himself for hacking the clinic's computer. He claimed he had no idea about Hyde's secret prison."

"A good 'soldier.' Anything on who totaled my car?"

"Not yet. And get this, both Peters and Hyde swear they weren't in your house."

"One of them is lying."

"That's what I thought." Tyler didn't sound convinced. "They've been lying about lots of stuff, this, I'm not sure."

"Wow, just great. There's another psychopath after me? Hyde still claiming he was the one who got attacked?"

"Like you wouldn't believe it. We'll figure it all out. I'll have another go at him tomorrow."

"I want to be there."

"Luce, that's impossible."

"Not in the room," she clarified. "I know that's not a good idea, though maybe he'd get angry and slip up. Anyway, I want to observe. I think I can help."

"I appreciate that, but...Don't you think you should take a break? You won't be back officially for a few days."

"There's no danger with me being in the observation room. I'll clear it with Chomsky."

"All right then. I'm glad you're doing okay."

That was debatable, but she didn't correct him. Awkward silence ensued once more.

"Thanks. Just in case she says no...I wouldn't be able to do that, obviously, but try to appeal to his ego. Pretend you're somewhat sympathetic to his cause."

"It's a bit nauseating to think about, but I see where you're going with this."

"He is so fucking proud of himself, he will tell you all of it."

"I can't wait." The sarcasm came through quite clearly. "You take good care of yourself and let me know if you need anything in the meantime."

"Thank you. I appreciate it. I mean it," she felt the need to add.

"I know. I'll see you tomorrow then."

"Fingers crossed."

⁓

Kendra set the table in the living room, both of them aware that Luce wasn't going to move a lot tonight. The casual set-up was welcome, though she was very much looking forward to them having romantic dinners together, sometime in the future.

The delivery service arrived not much later. When she saw what Kendra had decided, her jaw dropped.

There was Thai, Italian, burgers and Fish & Chips, all of it with sides.

"I know you found it difficult to choose. So, you don't have to, at all."

Much as she tried, Luce couldn't keep her mind from wandering back to the room, the small bowl of soup and that apple. That, and the fact that he kept the women on that ridiculous diet for days, weeks in some cases. They should have been indulging safely in cravings. Pregnant or not.

"Thank you."

She didn't have any more words, but Kendra seemed all right with a close embrace.

⁓

In the morning, she had taken the time to call her mother. Hearing her voice made Luce more emotional than she cared to admit. Fortunately, the press coverage so far hadn't gone into much detail, so, neither did Luce.

"So, Jill and Josie will come to visit after my renovations are done, and I wanted to ask if you'd like to join us."

"Of course. It will be fun. I miss you."

"I miss you too. But I've got to go now—"

"Are you really okay? You know, I could get on a plane..."

"No, please. I'm staying with a friend, and the house is still a mess."

She wasn't ready to have all the conversations, and at the moment, Luce was worried she might just blurt out things she wasn't ready to share yet.

"I really do have to go. I'll call again soon, I promise."

Then she could no longer stall. It was time to leave for the station.

Kendra followed her to the door, handing her the car keys.

"Are you sure you don't want me to drive you? I could just wait..."

"No, thank you. I'll be fine."

Luce accepted her embrace, stayed in it as long as she could justify. She didn't want to be late.

⁓

Half an hour later, she stood in her supervisor's office, as ready as she'd ever be.

"Allen, you look..." Luce's gaze must have warned her, because Lieutenant Chomsky caught herself. "Better than the last time I saw you. You know there's no way I can have you in the room with Hyde."

"I'm aware. I just want to observe. Maybe I can help Detective Murphy."

"I think he's perfectly capable, but since you're here, yes, you can observe. After that, I want you to go home and take the time you need."

"I will."

"I'm serious," Chomsky warned. "You have given this case everything. Those women are home safe now."

"Except Layla?"

"She will be in a few days. You saved her life."

"Me and Rachel."

"Yes, but take your share of the credit, will you?"

She might have wanted to say more, but after a knock on the door, D.A. Troy entered the room.

"Lieutenant...Detective Allen, good morning." She, too, did a bit of a double take. "How are you?"

Luce reminded herself of Kendra's words. Still, she was wondering how many more times she would have to answer that question. So far, so good, aside from those small freak-out moments.

"I'm good, thank you."

Tyler came in behind Troy.

"Hyde's here. Everyone ready to get started?" He gave Luce a quick smile in greeting. This, it felt good. Normal. She wasn't fooling herself.

Chomsky's phone rang, and she gestured for them to go ahead without her. Tyler went into the interrogation room, and Luce found herself alone with Troy.

They watched in silence as Tyler sat across from Hyde, leaning back in his chair, the two men sizing each other up. Luce suppressed a sigh.

"I never really apologized to you," she said. For the sake of closure... "I still think there's a danger in all of this, junk science, prejudice, accept it as an opinion."

"You're doing it again, Allen," Troy returned, sounding amused.

Luce glanced at Hyde as she wrapped her arms around herself. The warmth she'd felt in Kendra's home and company was fleeting. She could still feel the scratchy blanket against her naked legs, an insufficient protection.

"Well, I meant to say I won't have that conversation anymore. Here, in this context. You know where I stand."

"I sure do." After a small pause, Troy added, "For what it's worth, I'm sorry for what happened to you. This is not what any of us wants. He's a psychopath."

Luce remained silent. She had to focus on her self-imposed task. She wouldn't convince Troy that systemic prejudice allowed someone like Hyde to emerge, not today, maybe not ever. She didn't have the energy for it.

"I don't know what else you want, Detective," Hyde said. "All of them were about to make a mistake they were likely to regret for the rest of their lives. I wanted to help them, and I believe I did."

"It's a good thing there's no way he can plead insanity," Troy commented. "He did a lot of planning...but this sounds pretty insane to me."

"Help them how? You are not a doctor."

"Oh, please, we both know that most women manage just fine. It's nature."

"Yet, Wendy Tillis is dead. Layla Dorman miscarried," Tyler reminded him. "You didn't have enough supplies, medical or food. I fail to see how any of your actions were helpful."

Luce shook her head. "He's too antagonistic. That will only make Hyde shut down."

"Hyde isn't stupid. No matter what we tell him, he knows we don't approve of his actions."

She didn't feel like arguing with Troy and focused her attention on the interrogation instead.

"Detective, you know what I'm talking about. Maybe there was a lesson in it for them. If they hadn't intended to murder their babies in the first place, they wouldn't have been in that situation."

Luce gripped the back of the chair, needing something to keep her from fleeing the room.

"All I'm saying is you weren't very successful. And the detective? That was just because she was on to you. You had someone break into her house to scare her away."

Hyde smiled. Luce cast a quick sideways glance at Troy, seeing disgust in her expression, mirroring her own.

"Not exactly. Okay, I needed more time. I'll admit I didn't act fast enough at first, but I meant to give her back what she lost. What you both lost."

For a second or so, it seemed like everyone was holding their breaths.

"Come on," Luce muttered.

"You're right," Tyler said. "That was difficult. It's not something you forget easily."

"I understand. I bet you were angry at her. Mad enough that you wanted her to pay for what she did."

"If I was...Well, that's not something we can say out loud these days, can we?"

There was a minute change in Hyde's demeanor. Tyler had noticed it too. As chilling as this exchange was, Luce knew he had found the right angle.

"Our freedoms are taken away left and right," Hyde agreed. He laughed. "Left and right, that's almost funny, isn't it? Even our own elite doesn't like to be politically incorrect anymore. But the ones who support me never once thought I was too radical. They like what I have to say, that I'm telling it like it is. Your girlfriend? She was lucky. A few states away, my peers are going for the death penalty."

Lieutenant Chomsky had quietly entered the observation area. She remained standing, leaning against the door as Tyler continued.

"None of us can come back from that. You, at least, tried some form of rehabilitation."

"You could call it that."

"Still. Wendy Tillis."

Hyde shrugged. "There are casualties in every war, you understand that, Detective, don't you? All Wendy had to do is keep her head down and have her baby. It wasn't personal."

"I see. But you had her medical file. You knew she wasn't going to have an abortion, and you still kept her on that list?"

"She got very crass. I knew that she had been giving money to my opponent as well, the one who supports the killings."

"I see." Tyler kept a neutral expression. "The others, they didn't respect your policies. I heard things got a little out of control when you campaigned door to door."

"I was polite. I always was. Rachel was far too haughty."

"It's a good strategy, pretending to sympathize," Liz Troy said.

Luce nearly laughed. Worried it might sound mad, she suppressed the urge, though for once, she agreed. Her instincts were still working.

"Layla wasn't on the list," Tyler mused. "She was with you the longest."

"Bitch flirted with everyone. Men, women...but she didn't even notice me."

"I get it. No one wants to be disrespected."

"Maybe not, but few of us do something against it. Most of those so-called modern, progressive men cower. Like you."

"Excuse me?"

"You think you're the only one who did his homework? Your ex-wife cheated on you. Your girlfriend cheated you out of the opportunity to be a father. Yet you did nothing. Those ungrateful bitches learned a lesson. The world will remember me." He turned to the two-way mirror as if knowing who was behind it.

"They will remember me. Isn't that so, Detective Allen?" he asked, sporting a self-satisfied grin.

Luce turned away and left. She had heard enough.

Chapter
Twenty-Six

S he waited by her desk long enough for Tyler to finish the interrogation. They met in the briefing room with Chomsky and Troy.

"Nice work, Detective Murphy," Chomsky said.

"Thanks, but I can't take all the credit. Detective Allen gave me some excellent tips last night."

If that sounded ambiguous to anyone in the room, no one mentioned it.

"I appreciate the results, but please remember that Detective Allen is off the clock for now."

"I'll keep that in mind. Speaking of which, do you need a ride?"

"No thanks. Kendra lent me her car this morning. Lieutenant...Thanks for letting me stay."

"Of course. Now take some time. And don't hesitate to let us know if you need anything."

Even Troy gave a small nod.

"Thank you. I'll be back as soon as I get the all-clear."

As she left, Luce walked past an office, surprised to see Cory Baldwin and Rachel Benson. Rachel jumped to her feet to open the door.

"Detective! How are you?"

"Much better than two days ago," she admitted shaking Rachel's hand.

"You?"

"Furious," Rachel said, the fire in her eyes leaving no doubt as to the truth of her words.

"Yeah, that too. You are all right here? Should I get anyone?"

"Detective Crayden has been very nice," Cory said. She sounded even younger than she was. "Thank you too. For getting us out."

"Well, Rachel here helped a lot. All of you had a part in it."

"But we couldn't have done it without you."

Without warning, she found herself hugged tightly by the teenager. Over Cory's shoulder, Luce caught Rachel's wry smile.

"I don't mind sharing the credit, but I swear I'll never cook soup again in my life."

"I think that's fine."

Spontaneously, Luce took a couple of business cards out of her purse. Pay it forward.

"My colleagues will be happy to provide you with all the resources you need, but if you ever want to talk..."

They both took the card. Rachel's gaze was pensive, Cory's hopeful.

"Thanks. See you," Rachel said.

On her way home, Luce stopped by the hospital. Layla Dorman was asleep when she arrived, so she simply left the chocolates from the gift shop with a nurse.

Ritter looked pleased to see her.

"Allen, what the hell? I'm out for a few days and you solve the case?"

"Thanks, I think."

"Well done," he said, sounding sober. "The doc told me what happened. Damn."

"Yeah. Not only is my house still not finished, now I need a new car."

"At least you're up and running. Well, metaphorically speaking." he said. "I can't wait to go home too."

"I can imagine. They told you when?"

"Tomorrow if I'm lucky."

"Is there anything I can get you?"

"Thanks, but no. Betty is coming back later. I hear they think Hyde wasn't the one who broke into your house?"

"I don't know. He's probably lying."

"Yeah. I'm glad you're all right."

She left before he had the chance to correct his impression. Up and running, maybe. All right? That would have to wait.

❦

Luce meant to go home after that, but when she drove past a coffee shop, realizing it was the first time in a long time she had no obligations for a while to come, she parked in the lot and went inside. After she'd ordered a high-calorie, high-priced concoction, she went to a table by the window and sat down, enjoying the warmth of the sun.

It was over.

Some might sympathize with Hyde, politicians of a certain ilk would always try, but for him, this was the end of the line. She, and the other women, would get to enjoy a sweet treat in the afternoon, the safety of their own homes, share time and space with someone who cared about them. And no matter what reasoning he made up in his twisted mind, they deserved all of it.

Her gaze fell on a store window on the other side of the street, the sight making her smile. She added one more errand to her list.

After Luce had finished her coffee, she walked over to the store and asked the employee for the dress in the window.

While she was paying, her gaze fell on another one, her imagination taking her to a place in the future where she might have use for it. A time when the bruises wouldn't show so much any longer, and...

"I'm going to take that one too," she said.

The woman gave her a surprised but pleased smile.

"I'll go get it for you."

<hr />

Luce hadn't expected to be this exhausted, but when she arrived at Kendra's house, she could barely stand any longer.

A glass of water and a couple of pills appeared right in front of her moments later.

"Thank you, but wouldn't this be one of those days where a glass of wine is an acceptable remedy?"

"Tomorrow, maybe. Try these first. You were out for a while. How did it go?"

Luce leaned back into the cushions, suppressing a sigh. "It was...something, to witness Tyler and Hyde discuss the depravity of modern women."

"The approach you suggested worked though."

"Yeah. I knew it would."

She flinched at the sound of the doorbell.

"I'm not expecting anyone," Kendra said as she got up. "Let me go take a look?"

Luce heard her open the door and speak to the visitor.

"Luce? Could you come here for a second?"

She would have preferred to stay on the couch. Nevertheless, she was curious. When Luce saw who was standing on the other side of that threshold, she was surprised that the door was still open.

"Detective, I was told I could find you here."

"By whom?" Kendra asked, her tone dripping with sarcasm. "One of those genius hackers your organization employs?"

"Could I come in for a moment? I was hoping I could talk to you."

Luce was tired of being the bigger person, had been for some time, when it came to these kinds of conversations. She was also even more curious. Maggie Rowland? What did she want?

"This is Dr. Jones's home. It's up to her if she wants to invite you in."

Kendra shrugged. "Did you bring a gun?"

"No, I swear," Rowland said, as if that was to be expected. "I just wanted to let you know I heard, about…Mr. Hyde and what he did."

Kendra excused herself and went to the kitchen but remained in Luce's line of vision as she and Maggie went to sit in the living area.

"I guess everyone has heard by now."

"It's abominable," Maggie said with surprising vehemence.

"You really think so?"

For a moment, Luce thought she saw anger flash in the woman's expression. She, too, looked tired, though Luce was far from cutting her a lot of slack yet. She remembered the shouts and the signs.

"I'm a mother. He let one of them die. They way he treated them..." She shuddered.

"I appreciate you expressing your feelings, but I have to wonder...The last time we spoke you were proud to be a member of The Defenders. You know what they did?"

She nodded, the defiance gone from her stance.

"I do know. It's the reason I'm no longer associated with them. I think I can find a better way to advocate for the unborn."

"No argument from me."

The Defenders would have a larger investigation coming their way.

Luce still wasn't sure why Maggie Rowland had sought her out. Atonement?

"I never wanted anyone to get hurt."

She might even be telling the truth, but she was sure going at it from a questionable angle.

"You want to do better? Do it. There are many mothers and children in desperate situations who need support." Luce could tell that Rowland was on the verge of arguing. Time to end the conversation. "Thank you for stopping by. I think you did yourself, and your children, a favor by leaving that group."

"Get well soon, Detective."

Luce closed the door behind her and returned to the living room, where Kendra had prepared a plate with appetizers from last night's leftovers. A couple of small glasses of wine sat on the table.

"Oh. Don't tell my doctor."

"I can keep a secret, Detective."

She was so grateful to sit. For the sip of wine, too. But most of all for Kendra who took it in stride that Luce's feelings for her were still all over the place.

Kendra sat next to her and kissed her forehead, a gesture both sweet and a promise of things to come. One of those better days that were in their future. Soon.

Chapter
Twenty-Seven

E ven if she had wanted to, she wouldn't have been capable of doing anything but fall asleep next to Kendra, temporarily safe in her embrace.

A glimpse of the future.

She wasn't spared a glimpse of what could have been, waking in a cold sweat from the nightmare. Hyde boasting about that stupid expensive wine and his plans.

"You want to get up for a bit? Get a glass of water?"

Luce couldn't deny that some water, and a change of PJs, might help.

"Maybe I should go back to my house for a bit," she said, because she didn't want to get into details of the dream. "There is so much to do."

"We can stop by tomorrow. I wasn't kidding when I said I wanted to help...and that you needed it."

Despite herself, Luce had to laugh. "I can always count on you to tell me the truth."

"Yes, you can. Now let's get that water."

They had stayed up for over an hour. To Luce's relief, the nightmare didn't return, but Kendra let her sleep in longer than she had in a long time.

She had also made plans, all dressed and ready to execute them when she walked into the bedroom.

"So, how about we drive over to your house, take a look at what still needs to be done, and who to call?"

"That might be a long list."

"It's all right. We have nothing else planned, right? If it's too much, we can always go back another time. And we'll get breakfast afterwards."

"Sounds good."

Luce couldn't help smiling. No matter the circumstances, neither of them was able to sit idly on a day off.

"Of course, after we come back, you'll get some more rest. Doctor's orders."

"Which doctor?" Luce teased.

"Come on. Let's go."

When they were in the car, Kendra turned on the radio to a station that played cheery pop music, which was more than all right with Luce. She had mixed feelings about going to the house, knowing that she couldn't avoid it and hide out at Kendra's forever.

It seemed like forever ago that she had started on those renovations—already working on Ashley Johnson's case. Before that visit to Jill's where she ran into Tyler again.

She wasn't looking forward to seeing those letters, even knowing that the person who had scrawled them onto her wall was wrong, a criminal, someone who had no room to judge.

That kind of thing would continue too, women being followed to their homes, intimidated, their personal information exposed. Fighting the tide was a Sisyphean task. But she'd continue to do it. Like Kendra.

Luce opened the door with her keys, letting her in first before she stepped inside.

Nothing much had changed. Kendra was right, she had to finish what she'd started with so much hope and enthusiasm...Luce stopped cold when she realized she was looking at a pristine light blue wall. No letters. There was nothing left of the intrusion.

She spun around, seeing Kendra smile.

"It wasn't me," she said. "Tyler was there when I talked to Ritter about the keys. He wanted to help."

Luce didn't know what to say.

"I didn't think he was going to..." She turned to the flawless wall again. "This looks good."

"He's that kind of guy. I also suspect he wants to stick around a bit longer, see how you're doing."

Luce shrugged. "I could have told him about the pregnancy," she said. "Either way, I'm glad the case is over."

"Yes, me too. So, what is going to happen in here? Were you going to do just the downstairs, or upstairs too?"

"I think downstairs is all I can handle for now, but I wanted an open floor plan."

"I see." Kendra regarded their surroundings with interest. "So, this wall is going to come down, right?"

Luce decided there was a fabulous metaphor in Kendra's question.

She stepped forward and pulled her close for a kiss, deeper and more passionate than they'd kissed before.

That wall would come down eventually, but she didn't want to wait any longer for those better days.

Judging from the way Kendra kissed her back, neither did she.

And perhaps that romantic date, for which she could wear her recent purchase, wasn't too far in the future.

Angelica had barely moved from her side since Cory returned. She was with her, too, when Mrs. Meyers knocked on the door to tell her that a package had arrived for her.

Who could it be from? People had been kind to her since she'd escaped from the madman, but this was strange.

"It's from that store you were looking at," Angelica was stating the obvious.

"I know." Cory opened the bag, her jaw dropping when she saw what was in it: That dress she had been dreaming about but could have never afforded. She got gifts for her birthday and Christmas, but never anything this expensive.

"Wow," Angelica commented.

"Yes, wow." She reached into the bag to produce a small card.

I know it can't make up for everything that happened, but Angelica told me you liked it...I thought you should have it. Enjoy. Luce

Cory read the message through blurry eyes.

"You want to try it on?"

"Yes. Yes, I want to."

Luce Allen was right. It wouldn't make her nightmares go away. This dress wouldn't magically turn her life around, but after escaping the man who had told her she deserved nothing—damn it, she deserved it.

He was sitting alone at the bar, nursing a beer, so engrossed in the activity he didn't see her coming. He didn't turn to her when she sat on the barstool next to him.

"Bad day?" she asked softly.

Joe Danes moved towards her so quickly he nearly fell off the chair. Luce was certain he knew who she was. In the aftermath of Hyde's arrest and the horror story unfolding, her face had been all over the news.

"Haven't you had a few of those in a row?" he asked, snickering.

The bruises in her face had been fading.

"That's true. But today is pretty great. Joe Danes, you're under arrest for the abduction of Ashley Johnson. Turn around—"

She knew he was gauging his chances, perhaps push her aside and run. Good luck with that. She wasn't going to let him do any of it.

"You heard her," Ritter said from behind him, and Danes let out an expletive.

As Luce put the cuffs on him, the bartender who had helped them set up the sting, smiled. Luce smiled back at him.

"You know, I promised Ashley, and myself, that you weren't going to get away. Today I get to keep that promise."

"Don't mess with her," Ritter said. "Never a good idea."

More important—as of tonight, many more girls and women were out of harm's way.

The woman she had fallen for, hard, was waiting for her at home.

Yes, this was one of the best days in a long time.

About the Author

B arbara Winkes writes sapphic crime drama and Christmas romance. She loves writing characters who get the job done, whether it's stopping a predator or saving cherished traditions—while still making time for love. She lives with her wife in Quebec, Canada.

barbarawinkes.com

Also by Barbara Winkes

The Crossing Lines Trilogy
Undercover
Redemption
Vengeance

The Connected Series
Promised to the Queen
Drawn to the Enemy
Tempted by the Protector

Kelli & Merin Romantic Suspense
Thunder
Rain

Standalone
The Amnesia Project

www.ingramcontent.com/pod-product-compliance
Lightning Source LLC
Chambersburg PA
CBHW030307200626
46816CB00002BA/802